"What's wi... Brooke sta... perplexed. "Are you a compulsive gambler or something?"

Garrett raised his brows. "Or something. I'm not afraid to take chances once in a while, if that's what you mean. How about this—I'll bet I can get cozy with your cats before you can make friends with my dogs. Name your own stakes. Make it easy on yourself." He gave her a knowing wink.

She recoiled in horror. "No way!"

He ignored her protest. "So, what are the stakes? Hey, I've got it! This is a B and B, right? How about the winner gets breakfast in bed?"

Dear Reader,

Welcome to our exciting showcase series for 1997!

Authors you'll treasure, books you'll want to keep!

Harlequin Romance books just keep getting better—and we enjoy bringing you the best choice of wonderful romances each month. Now, for the whole year, we'll be highlighting a particular author in our monthly selections—a specially chosen story we know you're going to enjoy, again and again....

This month's recommended reading is Ruth Jean Dale's *Breakfast in Bed*, a charming book full of fun and humor. Our SIMPLY THE BEST title for August will be *Wild at Heart* (#3468) by Susan Fox.

Happy reading!

The Editors

Breakfast in Bed
Ruth Jean Dale

Harlequin Books

TORONTO • NEW YORK • LONDON
AMSTERDAM • PARIS • SYDNEY • HAMBURG
STOCKHOLM • ATHENS • TOKYO • MILAN
MADRID • WARSAW • BUDAPEST • AUCKLAND

For my daughter, Valerie Duran,
a world-class reader of romance—
and everything else she can get her hands on!

ISBN 0-373-03465-2

BREAKFAST IN BED

First North American Publication 1997.

Printed in U.S.A.

CHAPTER ONE

OH, CLARENCE, our love can never be, for you are promised to another....

Brooke had to blink away tears so she could read the elaborate script of the silent movie title card flickering on the enormous television screen. Not that she actually needed to *read* the words; she'd seen the film so many times that she knew it, and them, by heart.

Forbidden Love, filmed in 1925, had been the first movie to star the sixteen-year-old Cora Jackson. Decades later, her luminous celluloid beauty still transfixed twenty-five-year-old Brooke Hamilton, companion of the former movie star's old age.

The glorious child-woman wafted gracefully across the shadowy screen. Brooke's hand stilled on the back of the sleek orange cat draped across her lap—Miss Cora's cat, one of two left in Brooke's care under the terms of the will. Watching the woman's first film on the VCR two months after her death, Brooke still found it impossible to believe that her friend and mentor was really gone. Even well into her eighties, Miss Cora had remained a vital and captivating woman.

The cat stirred, casting Brooke a disapproving glance over one furry shoulder. "Sorry, Gable," she apologized, resuming a slow stroking. "I know I get carried away, but I miss her so much. I'll bet you do, too." She swallowed hard and read the next title card.

5

For honor's sake, you must marry another upon the morrow. But you will always be my only love—no, don't look at me so!

The on-screen Cora, the one who would remain forever young and beautiful, pressed the back of a slender wrist against her mouth dramatically, tears sparkling like diamonds on her lashes. Many times Miss Cora had explained to the enraptured Brooke that in those days of silent films, cameramen had moved heaven and earth to photograph stars in the best possible light.

"It took onions to get those tears to come and a genius with a camera to make them look sincere," Cora insisted. "Goodness, what did I know about acting? Talent didn't even enter into it. I was just a little girl from Illinois who found herself in Hollywood."

That fortuitous circumstance had changed Cora's life, and more than a half century later, Brooke's life, as well. "Go figure," she mused to Gable, tickling his ear with a gentle fingertip.

He responded with something that sounded vaguely like "Arough-ooo!" Brooke glanced down at him in surprise to find him staring at the door as if he expected something dreadful to spring through at any second and attack him.

The door, like everything in Glennhaven, Miss Cora's magnificent Victorian mansion on a mountainside overlooking Boulder, Colorado, was dark and elaborate and reminiscent of days gone by. Brooke had come here today ostensibly to "sort and organize," but had found the prospect so depressing that she'd slipped a tape into the VCR instead.

She should have known that it would turn out to be a mistake. This house had been a second home to her, but she'd tried to avoid it since the death of the woman who'd been more family to her than her own family had ever pretended.

Cora Jackson Browne—Brooke's beloved Miss Cora—had been like a mother to her. Or perhaps the proper term was grandmother, since the woman had been at least sixty years older than her young companion. Her death was even more shocking because it had been completely unanticipated. She'd simply gone to bed one night and never awakened. Although it was a gentle end to a memorable life, Brooke had been devastated.

And more so when she realized that Miss Cora herself had somehow seemed to sense that her time was near. In a long and detailed letter written only a few weeks earlier but not found until after her death, she'd laid out her plans and expectations.

A simple burial; no members of her family to be notified of her death until just before the reading of her will; and custody of her cats to Brooke, along with an acre of land and the guest house.

In typical Miss Cora fashion, she'd been specific in every detail. Although not all of it made sense to Brooke, she was prepared to move heaven and earth to accommodate her beloved patron.

Thus she had steeled herself to come today to Glennhaven to begin the bittersweet task of organizing Cora's possessions, pending the eventual arrival of the new owner of this magnificent aberration. Miss Cora had entrusted Brooke with this chore, along with

many others. She was glad to do these final insignificant tasks but it was hard—

Gable stiffened and sat up on Brooke's lap. His ears
pointed toward the door, which was slightly ajar, then
slicked back flat against his broad head. Flexing his
claws into the tough fabric of her jeans, he arched up
on tiptoe.

"What is it, boy?" She tried to distract him by
rubbing his tummy, which usually worked but this
time fell flat. "Do you hear something?" She couldn't
imagine how, over the swelling strings of the musical
accompaniment to the sad tale of love and sacrifice
unreeling on the television screen.

Every bright hair on the cat's body stood on end.
Brooke, more curious than alarmed, followed the path
of his hostile glare.

"What is it, Gable?" She tried again to soothe him.
"There's nobody in the house but you and me—"

The door flew open with a resounding crash and
Brooke stared at the creature standing there—a dog!
A small, black-and-white, terrier-looking creature
who seemed to be all fangs and claws. What in the
world was a *dog* doing inside Glennhaven, the refuge
of all creatures feline?

Gable, for one, wasn't interested in hanging around
to find out. With an awful screech, he bolted from
Brooke's lap. The sudden movement startled the little
dog and he let out a yelp of alarm, quickly followed
by a staccato yapping that scared the woman almost
as much as the cat.

With a shriek of alarm, Brooke leapt to her feet.
The terrier didn't even seem to notice her, too intent

upon poor Gable, hotfooting it across the room. The straightest path between dog and cat, unfortunately, led through Brooke. Without hesitation, the dog took it.

Brooke panicked. In her haste to escape, she leapt in the wrong direction and one of her feet came down on the dog's paw. He let out a howl, which further unnerved her.

So did the deep and unfamiliar voice coming from the hall outside. "Larry? Larry, where are you, you miserable hound?"

The cat made it to the fireplace and, without pausing, leapt to the top of the broad mantelpiece. Once there, he turned to face his attacker. Gable's normally placid face wore a savage expression and he arched his back like a Halloween cat.

The dog, Larry, gave one final indignant yelp and threw himself at the fireplace, plowing into the elaborate stained-glass screen. It tottered, then fell, shattering on the hearth. The dog took no notice, too busy flinging himself into the air, trying—and failing—to reach his furry orange target.

And he yipped, and he yapped, making so much racket that Brooke wanted to scream. Instead, she turned and ran toward the door. She needed a weapon: a broom, a mop, anything to drive off that horrible creature threatening Cora's beloved Clark Gable.

Instead of finding help, she found herself face-to-face with a stranger. He looked as startled as she—and then she found herself in his arms, unable to halt her forward momentum.

He held her easily against his broad chest. A whiff

of his faint, woodsy aftershave surprised her, as did the strength of his impersonal embrace. Then he stood her on her feet and looked at her with a slightly puzzled smile curving his lips.

While she...stared. He was *gorgeous,* from his thick, midnight-dark hair to golden-hazel eyes alight with intelligence and curiosity. There was strength in the high cheekbones and square jaw, but humor in the quirk of the lips and tilt of his eyebrows when he looked at her.

And then she realized that blasted dog was still yapping and trying to climb up the fireplace to kill Miss Cora's innocent cat, who'd been minding his own business prior to this vicious and unprovoked attack.

"Is that your dog?" She almost gasped the words while pointing a trembling finger. "Make him stop!"

The handsome stranger frowned. "Yeah, what's got him so worked up?" His gaze swung smoothly from Brooke to the barking dog, then up to the big orange cat hissing and spitting his fury from on high. He recoiled. "That's a cat!"

"Well, yes, of course it's a cat." Brooke edged around until the tall stranger was between her and the animals. She'd face any cat anytime, anywhere, but dogs sent her into shock—even quiet ones, which this one certainly wasn't.

"What's a cat doing here?" the man demanded. His golden eyes narrowed. "For that matter, what are *you* doing here—not that I object, you understand."

"I'm taking care of things until the new owner—" She stared at him while understanding dawned. "Oh, dear."

"Exactly." Smiling, he offered his hand. "I'm Garrett Jackson. And you must be...Brooke Hamilton?"

"Yes." She touched his hand with hers, too lightly to be called a handshake. She hadn't meant to be unfriendly but she felt a jolt of electricity at even that slight touch. Not too unusual in bone-dry Colorado, she assured herself; nothing to worry about. "Please," she pleaded, "will you do something about that dog? I don't think he can reach Gable but—"

"As in Clark?"

She nodded. "That barking is making a nervous wreck of me."

Garrett shrugged. "Guess I'm used to him." Kneeling, he snapped his fingers and spoke in a coaxing voice. "C'mon, Larry, old boy, come to papa."

Larry didn't do any such thing; in fact, after one derisive glance over his shoulder, he yipped louder.

"Larry! Get over here!" Garrett spoke firmly, pointing to the priceless Oriental rug upon which he knelt.

Larry didn't even bother to look around this time, just kept trying to scramble up the fireplace stones.

"Damn!" Garrett rose to his feet. "What's wrong with that mutt? He's obnoxious but he's never been *this* bad before."

"Maybe that's not Larry at all," Brooke couldn't stop herself from suggesting. "Maybe it's his evil twin."

Garrett laughed, little smile lines curving at the corners of his generous mouth. He was extraordinarily attractive when he smiled. Well, in all honesty, he was extraordinarily attractive when he didn't smile.

"Very funny," he admitted. "But I know how to handle him."

"This I've got to see," Brooke muttered dubiously. She glanced anxiously at Gable, who no longer seemed so much frightened as annoyed. In fact, he seemed as curious as she to discover what would happen next.

"You doubt me?" Garrett's golden eyes narrowed speculatively. "You wouldn't want to put your money where your mouth is, would you?"

"Huh?"

"Wanna bet?"

"Not a chance! I'm not a gambling woman." Too true; Brooke didn't take chances when she could avoid them. "All I want is for you to get that beast away from my cat."

"Okay, okay, I can take a hint." Stepping around her, he stuck his head into the hallway. He was wearing sky-blue shorts and a white T-shirt, with white leather sneakers. His body was as attractive as his face, which hardly seemed possible.

Or fair.

"Molly!" he called. "Will you come in here, honey?"

Brooke's brows rose. "Wife? Girlfriend? Significant other?"

His grin broadened, became almost challenging. "Daughter."

Brooke felt a little jolt of relief. "I see."

"You don't, but that's okay."

A small form appeared in the doorway and his smile became less predatory, more gentle. "There you are, sweetheart. Think you can call old Larry off the lady's cat?"

The little girl nodded gravely, then looked at Brooke with solemn curiosity. "Hello," she said. "My name is Molly Jackson."

"My name is Brooke Hamilton. I'm pleased to meet you, Molly."

"Thank you very much." Such a serious little thing; not so much as the hint of a smile. "I'm five years old," she continued. "How old are you?"

Brooke melted. The child was exquisite, dainty and blond, golden-eyed like her father. She waited a moment for Garrett to intervene; instead he simply looked interested so she said, "I'm twenty-five."

"That's almost grown-up," Molly observed.

Brooke stifled laughter. "Sometimes I wonder."

"Gart is thirty-two," the child offered.

"Gart?" Brooke glanced at the man beside her. "She calls you Gart?"

He shrugged. "She can't handle Garrett, for some reason." Kneeling before the child, he placed his hands on her shoulders. "Can you call Larry off now, Molly? That barking is driving us all nuts."

"Yes, sir." Snapping her fingers smartly, if silently, she said in an imperious tone, "Larry! Come, Larry! Come!"

Larry stopped yapping and cocked his head, his ears standing up straight. Then he turned and trotted back to his pint-size mistress.

All Brooke could see was the dog's vicious white

teeth and powerful jaws. Frightened, she edged around Garrett, always keeping him between herself and that creature. When the coast was clear, she darted to the fireplace to snatch Gable to safety.

The cat curled himself around her shoulder and neck, his expression indignant in the extreme. "Gee, Gable," she murmured, rubbing his chest. "I'm sorry. It's not my fault, honest."

Garrett rolled his eyes. "You're apologizing to a cat?"

The way he said *cat* sent a warning shiver down her spine. "Why not? I got him into this mess when I let him coax me into coming along today. Of course..." She glanced significantly at the broken glass, which was all that remained of the fire screen. "I'm not entirely to blame. Do you have any idea how much that piece of stained glass was worth?"

"No idea whatsoever." He looked around the room. "Or anything else in this mausoleum, for that matter. What a tomb!"

"A tomb!" Aghast, she stared at him. "It's not a tomb. It's a beautiful Victorian mansion brimming with fabulous old treasures and priceless antiques."

"I like young stuff myself." His glance skimmed over her lightly but insolently, head to toe. He had the most intimate way of looking at her, as if he already knew something she didn't. It made her wish she'd put on something more impressive than jeans and a plaid shirt this morning.

"You inherited very little *young stuff,*" she said tartly. "We're old-fashioned around here. We do, however, have telephones."

"Is that a crack?" If it was, he didn't appear to be put off by it.

"I wasn't expecting you until next week," she reminded him.

"I've been trying to call for four days, ever since Molly and I left Chicago." He ruffled the little girl's soft curls, but he was watching Brooke.

"You drove?" But of course they drove. How else would they be accompanied by that obnoxious little dog now licking his young owner's hand?

He nodded. "Had a nice time, too, didn't we Molly, old girl? The dogs were a bit of trouble but—"

"Dogs, as in plural?" She glanced around with fresh alarm. "You mean, there's more than one?"

"Had to bring old Baron." He gave a whimsical shrug. "He's a German shepherd and not nearly as noisy as Larry."

Brooke couldn't stifle her groan. "I suppose he bites first and asks questions later."

Garrett frowned. "Are you trying to tell me you don't care for dogs?"

"I'm trying to tell you that I don't see how *anybody* could care for dogs. They're big and mean and they bite people and dig holes and—" she glanced significantly at the shattered glass on the hearth. "—break things."

"Unlike cats," he inserted smoothly, "who are little and mean and sneaky, with sharp teeth and claws made for shredding furniture and clothes—"

"Of all the nerve!" She glared at him, instinctively clutching Gable more tightly. That ungrateful wretch responded by jerking away. Leaping from her shoulder onto the cut-velvet sofa, he proceeded to dig his claws into the upholstery even as she defended him from such scurrilous charges.

Garrett's quick smile was mischievous. "Sorry, I got carried away. I take back the part about the furniture."

She gave him a sheepish grin. "Apology accepted." She added, "Stop that, Gable!"

"Can I pet your cat?" inquired an anxious little voice.

Brooke glanced from the child to the father, asking a question with her eyes. *Is it all right*?

He nodded. "But first let me put Larry out into the hall."

"Good idea." Brooke drew Molly forward. "Did you ever have a cat?"

The little girl shook her head. There was something so solemn about her, as if she didn't laugh nearly enough. "Only dogs," she said. "I got Larry when he was a little puppy."

Brooke's heart sank. Molly's ownership would give that miserable mutt privileged status. "Cats are nicer," she said staunchly. "Now, you must remember never to try to grab a cat. They don't like that. You have to make them think that everything's their own idea...."

Slowly and smoothly she reached for Gable, who permitted himself to be lifted from the couch and into Brooke's familiar embrace. "Sit down," she instructed the little girl, "and I'll put him on your lap. If you don't startle him, he may decide to stay. But if he wants to go, don't try to hang on to him, okay?"

"Okay." Molly sat down on the sofa, sliding back until her legs were straight out before her on the wide cushion. Carefully she smoothed her blue cotton skirt over her lap, then looked up expectantly.

Brooke leaned close to Gable's ear. "You be nice now, you hear?" she murmured. Gently she deposited the cat on Molly's lap.

Gable sank down like a puddle of orange pudding, turning his head to look into Molly's eyes with a "How'm I doin'?" expression. Apparently satisfied with what he saw, he began to purr.

"He's making noises," Molly exclaimed, looking up at Brooke anxiously.

"That's because he likes you," Brooke interpreted. "You can scratch his ears, if you're very gentle, or underneath his chin. He likes that."

"*I* like *him*," Molly declared fiercely. "Oh, Gable!" Unable to restrain her enthusiasm, she leaned forward and gave him a big hug.

Which was way too much for any self-respecting cat. He slipped out of her embrace as quickly and easily as smoke from a clenched fist. Before she could recover, he'd shinnied up the heavy brocade drapes to perch atop a tall bookcase.

Molly looked close to tears. "Make him come back," she pleaded.

Brooke slipped her arm around the child's shoulders and gave her a comforting squeeze. "I can't, honey. Nobody can make cats do anything they don't want to do. The trick is to make them think you don't really care, and that what *you* want them to do is really what they *want* to do."

Garrett, leaning against the closed door with his arms crossed over his chest, gave a derisive peal of laughter. "Are we talking about cats here, or women?"

Brooke pursed her lips. "Very funny."

"So are you, if you think I don't mean it."

"Are we talking about women here, or cats?"

"Touché!" His laughter this time sounded delighted. "Although I know as much as I care to know—about cats." He gave an exaggerated shudder. To Molly, he added, "We don't have time for cats now anyway. You said you were hungry, so let's see if we can find the kitchen. If we do, maybe we'll also find something for you to eat."

Brooke felt a little fissure of alarm. "It's after one o'clock. Are you saying this child hasn't had lunch?"

He shook his head. "But that's all right. There's probably something around…anything at all. We're not particular."

"There's not a bite to eat in this house." Why did he have to look so…pitiful? "The cook cleaned everything out of the kitchen before she left."

"Ouch." He crossed to Molly's side. "I guess that means we'll have to drive all the way down the mountain to feed you, you poor little thing."

Brooke was being set up and she fought it. "If you had called, I could have stocked the kitchen for you," she said defiantly.

"I tried—didn't you hear what I said before? I think the telephone lines must have been down or something."

Brooke groaned. He *had* mentioned that. Although

she didn't know of any trouble, the telephone service way up here in the middle of nowhere was so iffy that she never knew from one minute to the next if they had contact with the outside world. Knowing she shouldn't, she still heard herself saying, "Okay, if you meant it when you said you're not too particular, I suppose I could find *something* for—"

"Hey, thanks!" He didn't even wait for her to finish the invitation. Grabbing Molly by the hand, he lifted her to her feet.

"But no dogs," Brooke said sternly. Picking up the television remote, she clicked off the set before facing him. "You and Molly can come but *no dogs.*" Maybe that would dissuade him; she could but hope.

Instead of objecting, he nodded. "I've got food for the dogs," he said cheerfully. "It's Molly and me who are starving, right, sweetheart?"

The little girl nodded, keeping all her attention focused on Brooke, who knew when she was licked.

There was nothing to do but coax Gable down from his perch and onto her shoulder, then lead the invaders to her own sanctuary.

Which, she had a strong premonition, would never be the same after Garrett Jackson invaded it.

Garrett hated to tie his dogs to a tree out front of his late great-aunt's moldy old mansion, but he really didn't have much choice. With the toothsome Ms. Hamilton looking on, he did the dastardly deed quickly and efficiently. When he turned back to his little audience of woman, child and cat, he'd have sworn the furry four-legged observer was smiling with evil satisfaction.

But he wasted little time or attention on the cat, much more interested in the woman. Brooke Hamilton, he thought with satisfaction, was quite an eyeful. Even so, he'd early on got the impression that she either didn't know that or didn't much care. For one thing she was dressed without even a nod to fashion, and if she wore a speck of makeup, he couldn't see it. That natural look wasn't something he had much experience with but he found it surprisingly appealing.

He liked the sleek and shiny brown hair framing an oval face with high cheekbones and a full, tenderly shaped mouth. Her brown eyes sparkled with a quick, intelligence, which simultaneously drew and repelled him—drew him because he appreciated wit where he found it, repelled him because past experiences with smart women had been...chancy. They tended to look beneath the surface of things, beneath the surface of *him*. That wasn't an experience he relished.

Garrett Jackson preferred the quick and superficial when it came to women and much else in his life. No strings, no regrets; easy come, easy go. Except for Molly, of course. He looked at the little girl, rising on tiptoes beneath an arbor of tangled vines to stroke that damned cat still cuddled in Brooke's arms.

Molly had been a little trooper on this trip. When they'd started out, he'd thought they could benefit from a little time alone together and he'd been right. Although she hadn't exactly turned into a chatterbox, she'd shown a lively interest in everything going on around her. He was grateful for that, and for anything else that helped pull her out of her shell.

Except cats.

"I'm ready when you are," he announced brusquely.

Brooke looked up with a quick smile. Damn, she had a beautiful mouth, curving and sweet and somehow vulnerable.

"Dogs all tied up?" she asked somewhat anxiously.

"Yeah, and I hated to do it. I hope you don't expect—"

"But I do," she said quickly, turning with that orange monstrosity still draped over her arm like a stole. "It's the only answer."

"What's the question?"

"How to keep your dogs and my cats separated, for openers."

"How hard can it be?" He fell in beside her on the path, made up of individual stones set into the earth with some kind of moss growing between. "We're only talking about two cats and two dogs, four animals in total."

"Not...exactly." She gave him what might have been an anxious glance.

He felt a prickle of apprehension. "Not...exactly?"

"I have a few more than two cats."

He groaned. "How many's a *few more*?"

"Well...four. Of my own, that is."

She hesitated at an ivy-covered gate, and he stepped forward to open it for her and Molly. Through a thick stand of pine, he caught a glimpse of their destination—actually the former gatehouse to Glennhaven. And as he knew too well, his crazy great-aunt Cora had left the gatehouse to Brooke Hamilton, along with an acre of land.

An acre of land in the shape of a pan, the "handle" providing access to the main road—and effectively controlling access to the main house and the bulk of the estate. The bequest to the lovely Ms. Hamilton had left the future of the estate in doubt; the whole situation was a mess. He figured Cora must have been a raving lunatic, or else Ms. Hamilton was not the wide-eyed innocent she appeared to be.

Then Brooke's possible meaning sank in. "Four cats of your *own*?"

She nodded. "Uh...I guess you don't know about my business."

"You run a business from the gatehouse?" This was getting worse and worse.

She turned onto a well-defined path leading through the trees, and again he fell in beside her with Molly trotting along behind. All of a sudden Brooke stopped and opened her arms for Gable—check that, for that damned cat—to leap to the ground.

"He's getting away!" Molly's voice turned shrill.

"Don't worry, honey." Confidently Brooke took the little girl's hand. "He'll just lead us back home. He likes running through the trees. I try to let him, when I'm there to watch out for predators." She shot a quick, veiled glance at Garrett.

"Can I run, too?" Molly looked from one adult to the other. "Can I, can I, please?"

Brooke deferred to Garrett. "Is it okay? The house

is right there, where we can see it. We'll be right behind her.''

He didn't like it but he liked the disappointment on Molly's face even less. Everybody was always telling him he was overprotective and maybe he was. With an effort, he began, ''If you're sure...''

That was enough for Molly, who took off with her thin brown legs flying. Brooke smiled at the sight.

Garrett watched for a moment before returning to the subject at hand. ''You were talking about your business,'' he prompted.

''Oh, that.'' Her smile was absolutely angelic. ''I run a bed-and-breakfast for—''

''Jeez, a B 'n' B?'' Garrett stared at her incredulously. ''Does that mean I can expect to find hordes of strangers wandering around at all times of the day and night?''

''Goodness, no.'' She laughed lightly but he saw her twist her hands together behind her back.

''Then, what?''

''It's not a B 'n' B for people,'' she said. ''I'll give you a hint. It's called Catty-Corner.''

Before that could sink in, she whirled and ran down the path after Molly and Gable. Garrett stared after her in a state of shock.

He'd just inherited an estate dedicated to the one animal on this earth traditionally despised by his entire family.

CHAPTER TWO

BROOKE tried to keep her reservations at bay as she showed her guests around Catty-Corner. Maybe Garrett wouldn't be as difficult about the cats as she feared, she decided in a burst of positive thinking. Maybe he'd give in gracefully.

Maybe pigs would fly.

Following her around the premises, he gave no indication of either approval or disapproval, although he did seem a bit more subdued than he had earlier. Even suspecting he was waiting for his chance to confront her, she still couldn't conceal her pride in what she'd accomplished.

"With Miss Cora's help and approval, of course," she added, opening a door and gesturing them through. "None of this would have been possible without her total understanding and support."

They entered a large, cozy room containing ten spacious kitty condos spaced against the walls with Brooke's work and storage area in the center. Each compartment had a private window for bird-watching—a popular pastime of the residents—and pet-door access to an enclosed and partitioned sunning porch for felines only.

Garrett stared, his expression incredulous. "You're kidding," he said at last.

Brooke hardly knew how to take that. "Certainly

24

not.'' She lifted her chin a notch. "What did you expect? Surely not *cages*!''

"That's exactly what I expected,'' he admitted.

She shuddered. "My business comes from cat lovers, not sadists.'' She slipped her fingers through the wire mesh to tickle the chin of a dainty black cat named Chloe.

His eyebrows soared. "Talk about pampered. What do you do, serve them breakfast in bed?''

"Sure, if that's what they want,'' she admitted.

"Lucky cats.''

She didn't like that gleam in his amber eyes. To change the subject, she took Molly's hand and smiled at the little girl. "I think it's time I found *you* something to eat.''

Molly hung back. "Can I pet the kitties? Can I, please?''

"Maybe later.'' Brooke cast a questioning glance at Garrett, then led the way back through the door into her own quarters. Cluttered and homelike, her sitting room boasted an eclectic blend of period and modern furniture, all chosen for comfort or sentiment. "Let's go out to the kitchen first,'' she suggested to Molly, "and see what we can—''

But she'd lost her audience. With a cry of delight, Molly darted forward with hands outstretched.

She'd spotted Carole Lombard snoozing in a fluffy white mass on a big brocaded ottoman. It was love at first sight. Carole Lombard, Miss Cora's other cat, was practically designed to enchant a little girl: a snowy-white feline beauty with brilliant blue eyes and fur as soft and luxurious as a rabbit's.

Lombard gave a little squeak of surprise but she didn't try to elude her young admirer. To Brooke's astonishment, the cat allowed the child to embrace her, then sit down on the ottoman and haul the languid feline into her lap.

"What's her name?" Molly asked breathlessly, her eyes shining like stars.

"Lombard," Brooke said softly. Why did this little girl have a *dog*? If Brooke had ever seen a child take to cats, this was the one.

"I love her," Molly said fervently.

Brooke smiled. "I kind of think she loves you, too. I'll call you when lunch is ready, honey."

Brooke turned again toward the kitchen, her smile lasting until she saw Garrett. "Uh...you can wait in here with Molly, if you like." She made the suggestion hopefully.

"I'd rather go with you." He gave her a lazy, provocative grin. "There are a couple of things we need to talk about."

Oh, dear, she thought, leading the way. *I don't think I'm going to like this.*

Garrett perched on a kitchen stool, watching Brooke prepare grilled cheese sandwiches and a big pitcher of lemonade. For some reason, his steady gaze made her feel uncharacteristically clumsy and uncoordinated.

He spoke suddenly, startling her. "How well did you know my great-aunt?"

"Very well—maybe better than anyone. I worked for her for almost four years." She rummaged around in a cabinet, finally extracting a cast-iron griddle, which she placed on the stove.

"What did you do for her, exactly?"

She shrugged. "Whatever needed doing. I took care of her cats, dealt with the staff—she had a cook, a housekeeper, a gardener and occasionally others in to do special things. Like...she had the rose garden dug up a couple of years ago and installed a glass-enclosed swimming pool."

His eyes narrowed slightly. "For whom? At her age, she surely didn't—"

Brooke's laughter stopped him. "You didn't know her or you wouldn't ask such a question."

"Meaning?"

"Miss Cora got tired of swimming at the health club," she said airily.

That drew an apparently reluctant smile from him. "She's beginning to sound like quite a character."

"You could say that." Talking about Miss Cora was soothing and Brooke began to feel less stressed. "I'm only sorry you didn't get a chance to know her."

"Did she tell you about..."

"About what?"

"The family scandal."

"No—but you make it sound really interesting." She cast him an oblique glance. "I didn't even know she had a family."

"She didn't—not much of one, anyway. I wasn't actually named in her will, I was just the only one *left* except for a few distant cousins."

"I'm glad there was someone," Brooke said sincerely. "I had no idea who the beneficiaries of her will were until after she was gone."

"But you did know she was leaving the gatehouse to you." He glanced around the sunny kitchen somewhat pointedly.

Brooke stiffened. "I certainly did not."

He looked less than convinced. "And I suppose you didn't encourage her to put those crazy restrictions in her will?"

She flipped a sandwich on the stovetop grill, exposing a golden-brown surface. "What crazy restrictions?"

"Crazy restrictions about selling."

She whirled, a tide of heat rising in her cheeks. "Selling! You can't sell it!"

"Want to bet?"

Biting her lip, she turned back to the stove, mashing the sandwiches so hard she squeezed out a big glob of melting cheese. "A member of Cora's family must live here or the house and grounds are to be given to the County of Boulder for a cat sanctuary," she said at last. "Those are the only two choices."

She heard him rise from his stool, heard his footsteps approach, then heard his heavy sigh from just behind her quivering shoulder blades. And then she heard his husky voice and felt tension tighten her shoulders.

"Don't be naive," he said. "I'm an attorney from a family of attorneys. I'm only going to be here long enough to find a buyer."

"Garrett—Mr. Jackson!" She turned to face him, her spatula held between them like a sword. "Surely you don't mean that. How could you live with your-self if you ignored your aunt's stated wishes in such a cavalier manner? You don't have a moral problem with that?''

He smiled. Up close like this, the force of his per-sonal magnetism hit her like a sledgehammer blow, knocking the breath right out of her.

"I have a problem, all right," he murmured.

"Thank heaven." Her shoulders slumped with re-lief.

"My problem," he said with slow deliberation, "is a bit more complicated than you seem to realize. You see, I've got to buy *your* house and land before I can sell mine. And that, Brooke Hamilton, is exactly what I intend to do."

She squared her shoulders and glared at him. "Never!"

"Never say never."

He caught her arms just above the elbows, his grip light but very sure. Leaning closer, he stared into her eyes as if he wanted to make absolutely certain she realized he meant business.

"But my cats—my home—" She stared back at him in horror but saw no softening of his attitude. "I'll never sell," she said finally. "I never asked for this place, certainly never expected it or anything else in her will. But Miss Cora wanted me to have it, to live here and do exactly what I'm doing. It would have made her very happy, I know it would."

"Cora's dead. I'm alive, and I'll pay you enough money to move the whole kit 'n' caboodle someplace else and turn a nice profit besides."

"I don't want to go someplace else," she objected desperately.

"Be reasonable, Brooke." His voice became lower, more intimate. "I don't know what the old lady was thinking of. The configuration of your land all but destroys the value of mine. Surely you don't want to deprive me of the highest and best use of my inheritance."

She stared at him mutely, feeling helpless before this reasoned, coaxing approach. His hold on her bare arms seemed to be sapping her strength and she was still having difficulty breathing. "I...but I don't..."

She had no idea how to deflect his arguments and might have stood there indefinitely stammering and shaking if Molly hadn't walked through the doorway with Lombard nestled in her arms.

The little girl sniffed the air. "What's burning?" she asked innocently.

"Omigosh!" Whirling, Brooke snatched the skillet from the stove—too late, unfortunately. One side of each sandwich was golden brown while the other was, in Molly's words, "Golden black."

But the spell had been broken, which was worth a bit of burned bread. While Brooke prepared a second batch of sandwiches, she seethed over Garrett's bombshell.

The obvious truth of the matter was that he didn't care about Miss Cora's wishes. He just wanted to make as much money as he could as quickly as he could and go back to Chicago. Nor did he care what happened to Brooke or the cats or anything or anybody else.

Garrett Jackson was *selfish,* that's what he was. She darted him a hostile glance where he sat at the center work island, in conversation with his child.

Unfortunately, he was also better-looking than a movie star and more electrifying than the local power company.

Brooke Hamilton finally had to admit that she was in a *lot* of trouble.

Brooke couldn't eat, not after Garrett's callous announcement of his intentions. She played with her food, although her guests seemed to be enjoying the simple meal.

Because she was so upset, she found herself watching him with a kind of suspicion normally foreign to her. She prided herself on being an honest, straightforward person who didn't jump to conclusions. Yet as she watched father and daughter together, she found herself jumping to a *lot* of conclusions.

Garrett, she quickly decided, was…different when he was concentrating on his daughter. It was a side of him obviously kept well-hidden under normal circumstances. But what kind of relationship did the two of them really have? Molly called him by his first name, for heaven's sake—or as close to his first name as she could get. That did not denote the kind of closeness he seemed to be seeking.

And then Brooke found herself concentrating on Molly, in an effort to keep her thoughts off Molly's father. There was something curiously…*sad* about the little girl. She was polite and attentive, but perhaps a bit quiet and even a little withdrawn. When she turned those beautiful long-lashed amber eyes on Brooke, something melted inside and Brooke found herself wanting to enfold the child in a loving embrace.

Where was Molly's mother?

Brooke pushed the question aside. If she wasn't careful, she was going to get sucked into the Jacksons's family circle despite her best efforts to the contrary.

Molly popped the last bite of sandwich into her mouth, daintily applied a paper napkin, dropped it on the counter and slid from her stool. "May I be excused, please?" she inquired. "The cats need me."

"You're excused." Garrett sounded indulgent. "But don't get too involved with that cat, okay? We'll be going back to our own house soon."

Molly frowned. "I think I like this house better," she said, her glance darting from her father to Brooke.

"Nevertheless…"

Molly understood. Sighing, she turned toward the doorway.

When she'd disappeared, Brooke said a heartfelt, "She's adorable."

"I think so, too." But he said it in a rather brooding manner.

She couldn't help adding, "Her mother…?"

"Is dead."

"Oh! I'm so sorry."

"Thank you." He touched a napkin to his mouth. "Lunch was terrific. Thank you again."

"You're welcome." She chewed on her bottom lip for a moment. "Garrett, what you said earlier about selling the estate—"

"I meant every word."

She sighed. "I see. I was hoping I'd misunderstood."

"You didn't. Look," he added a bit impatiently, "why don't we put off serious discussion until Molly and I have a chance to get settled?"

"Of course, if you say so, but—"

"There's plenty of time."

Rising, he stretched, flexing movements bringing the muscles of his upper arms into stark relief. He looked fit and firm and ridiculously attractive.

She began gathering up the plates to divert her attention. "I suppose you're right."

"I know I'm—damn!"

Startled, she looked back at him. He was staring at his feet with a horrified expression. When she looked down, she saw Gable twining around his ankles like a clinging vine.

She burst out laughing. "Gable must be having a nervous breakdown to get close to a *dog* person," she teased.

Garrett shuddered. "That's not it." He gave her a pained glance. "Animals like me. Even cats. I don't know why."

"Come on!" She couldn't help scoffing. "Cats are much more discriminating than that. I'm sure Gable doesn't like you any better than you like him. He's probably just trying to bug you."

"Then he's succeeding beyond his wildest dreams." Garrett slid back onto his stool and pulled his feet up to the first rung. Gable cast him a pained glance, then wandered off. The man looked relieved.

"I hate when that happens," he said. "I don't know why, but cats love me. The damn things won't leave me alone."

She rolled her eyes. "I don't think so."

"Want to bet?"

"What's with you and bets?" She stared at him, perplexed. "Are you a compulsive gambler or something?"

He raised his brows. "Or something. I'm not afraid to take chances once in a while, if that's what you mean."

She felt her hackles rise. "Meaning I am?"

He shrugged. "If the shoe fits…"

"It doesn't. I just don't see anything to be gained by…by taking crazy risks." She felt herself growing flustered and wondered why.

"Hey, betting on whether or not a cat's got any smarts is hardly the same as taking a crazy risk— especially if you have the courage of your convictions. How about this—I'll bet I can get cozy with your cats before you can make friends with my dogs. Name your own stakes. Make it easy on yourself." He gave her a knowing wink.

She recoiled in horror only partly mock. "No way!"

He ignored her protest. "So what are the stakes? Let me think…." He made a great show of entertaining a plethora of fleeting thoughts, at last sitting up straight with a snap of his fingers. "Hey, I've got it! This is a B 'n' B, right? How about the winner gets breakfast in bed?"

"How about—" And then she realized he was

laughing at her and her outrage evaporated. She finished lamely, "We forget the whole thing? Cats are not taken in by cheap tricks and neither am I."

"Meaning dogs are?"

"I don't know anything about dogs and that's more than I care to know."

"An unreasonable attitude if I ever—"

The mellow clang of the entry bell startled them both. Brooke hadn't realized how deeply he'd drawn her into the escalating confrontation until she was jolted out again.

Glad of the interruption, she headed through the parlor to the front door, Garrett at her heels. Elderly Grace Swann stood outside, tapping one foot impatiently. Her chauffeur stood two steps to the rear, holding her Maine coon cat in his arms and looking bored.

Brooke greeted one of her best customers with a big smile. "Hi, Mrs. Swann. I see you've brought Pookie for a visit. His room's all ready and waiting."

"I'd expect nothing less from you, my dear." The woman stepped inside, gesturing with an arm dripping with diamond bracelets. "Higgins, you know the way. Please see Pookie to his room."

Higgins rolled his eyes but not even a twitch marred the straight line of the man's mouth. He'd been with Grace Swann long enough to understand these things. The little woman stepped forward, bending to look the cat in the eye.

"Now, you be a good boy," she admonished fondly, rubbing his furry ears. Pookie regarded her with emotionless dark eyes.

The chauffeur said, without changing expression, "*Now,* madam?"

She sighed. "Now, Higgins."

With a nod of acknowledgment, he marched into the hallway, carrying the shaggy fifteen-pound cat as formally as he'd carry a silver tray.

Brooke heard Garrett mutter in a tone filled with awe, "What is it, a lion?"

Mrs. Swann also heard. "It's a cat, young man." She fixed him with a steely stare which dripped with disapproval. "A champion cat, as a matter of fact. May I inquire who *you* are?"

Brooke rushed to fill the breach. "This is Garrett Jackson, Mrs. Swann. He's Miss Cora's great-nephew and he's come to—"

"Garrett Jackson, is it? Then I know who he is and why he's come." Grace Swann glared at him. "I was Cora's dearest friend for fifty years, don't forget. I happen to know *everything.*"

"In that case, you're in a class all by yourself." Garrett stuck out his hand. "Pleased to meet you," he added, sounding sincere and looking boyishly attractive.

"Don't be too sure about that." She ignored the hand but a smile twitched around her mouth, as if she found him hard to resist. "Time will tell. It always does."

Garrett smiled. "Yes, ma'am."

The old lady's mouth twitched as if she were suppressing a smile. She turned to Brooke. "Have you any questions before I go, my dear?"

"Have there been any changes in diet or routine since Pookie's last visit?"

"None whatsoever."

"Then my only question is, how long will he be with us this time?"

"I'm not sure." Grace cocked her silver head thoughtfully. "The entire summer, most likely. I'm going first to visit family in Rhode Island and then to a film retrospective in Madrid. From there...well, I'm just not sure. I'll drop in from time to time to check on my angel, though."

"That's good. I give him a lot of attention but he still misses you."

Mrs. Swann looked pleased. "As well he should. You just be sure you take good care of him, dear." She turned toward the door. "He's my baby, bless his little heart. You know I wouldn't dream of leaving him with anyone except you, Brooksey."

"I appreciate that, Mrs. Swann." Brooke followed the woman outside where they lingered, waiting for Higgins to reappear.

Mrs. Swann leaned close to speak in a conspiratorial tone. "Keep Pookie away from that young man," she advised. "He's far too good-looking to be trustworthy, and I should know."

Brooke gave a little gasp of surprise, then realized she shouldn't be. Mrs. Swann might be pushing ninety but there was obviously a lot of life in the old girl yet.

Filled with curiosity, Garrett watched Brooke and the feisty little woman whispering together on the front porch. Not that he thought they were saying anything particularly interesting or relevant, probably just cat talk. But he'd always had an insatiable curiosity about everything and everyone he met.

Perhaps that was what made him a good attorney.

The chauffeur, Higgins, returned, collected his mistress, installed her in the gleaming Bentley parked in front and then drove slowly away. Only after the automobile had rounded a curve in the leaf-shadowed road did Brooke come back inside the house.

Putting his finger to his lips, Garrett pointed to his sleeping child, sprawled on a sofa with Carole Lombard for a pillow. Brooke's tight expression softened into a gentle smile.

What was it about women and children? Garrett wondered. If the way to a man's heart was through his stomach, then the way to a woman's heart must be through the nearest kid.

Since all was fair in love and war, he'd have to remember that.

She came close to him, presumably so she could speak softly to avoid disturbing the slumbering child. "I have to go check on Pookie," she whispered. "If you need to leave now—"

"I'm in no hurry," he said blandly. "I'll just wait, if you don't mind. Maybe make friends with a cat or two, just to show you I can and win our bet."

"*Your* bet." She made a soft, scoffing sound. "Don't bother—breakfast in bed is out."

"I can think of other prizes, if I absolutely have to."

"You're incorrigible."

"I find *you* very corrigible."

She gave him a slightly confused glance before turning away. He watched her through the doorway, then walked over to sit down gingerly on the very edge of the ottoman where Clark Gable lay napping. The cat opened one eye and gave the interloper a challenging glance before going back to sleep.

Ignoring the cat, which was the only way to treat the entire breed, Garrett watched Molly, still sound asleep. Since they'd be here for the better part of the summer, he supposed he should probably...explain her to Brooke.

In the meantime...he sighed and met the blue-eyed gaze of Carole Lombard. The white cat seemed to stare at him with a kind of lazy challenge. Garrett shivered and sucked in a deep breath. Cats. *Argh*!

The things he'd do to get his own way....

Brooke couldn't believe that Clark Gable would stab her in the back, yet when she reentered the sitting room she found the big orange cat draped across the lap of the enemy. Garrett was stroking the creature with great sweeping motions obviously perfected on some dog somewhere.

"What are you *doing*?" she demanded in an outraged whisper, starting forward to rescue her pet.

"Shh!" He glanced significantly at Molly. "Don't worry about old Clark, here. We're best buddies."

Another healthy stroke; a cloud of orange-and-brown-tipped cat hairs rose on a beam of light and sifted back down to settle on man and ottoman.

Brooke frowned. "What did you do to my cat?" she demanded. "Did you drug him?"

"This isn't your cat, it's his evil twin." Garrett gave back her earlier words, his eyes gleaming with mischief. "I told you, you can't trust cats. They just lay around waiting for a chance to make a fool of you. Dogs, on the other hand—"

Throwing up her hands in disbelief, Brooke turned and walked into the kitchen. What in the world was going on here? She didn't even know this man, yet her heart was pounding and her mind racing as if...as if she were really attracted to him.

Which, of course, she wasn't. He'd come here to dismantle an entire way of life left in his care by a wonderful woman he'd never even bothered to get to know. Brooke wouldn't, couldn't, let herself succumb to the temptations he presented.

Naturally, he followed her; he had a penchant for that. She gave him an unhappy glance. "So you used old Gable to make a point and then dumped him," she accused.

"Hey, that's life. Love 'em and leave 'em." He leaned his elbows on the center work island, resting his chin on his hands. The amber eyes he turned toward her sparkled with some indefinable devilry. "But you have to admit, cats love me. I won our bet hands down. That's the important thing."

"To you, maybe."

He looked surprised. "Winning's important to everyone, in case you hadn't heard."

"No, being *happy* is important to everyone."

"That's a woman's point of view."

"I *am* a woman, or hadn't you—" She stopped short, appalled. She knew he'd noticed she was a woman, and it was that knowledge which had her so on edge. Because *him* noticing made *her* notice, which left her somehow vulnerable.

He straightened slowly away from the counter. "I noticed, all right." A sexy little smile curved his lips. "You owe me a prize."

"I don't owe you a thing."

"Oh, yes, you do." He advanced on her, still slowly. "Nobody likes a welsher. You'll have to pay up."

Feeling like a bird hypnotized by a snake, she retreated, also slowly. "Stop right where you are, Garrett Jackson."

"I wanted breakfast in bed but you seem strangely reluctant to go for that," he reminded her. "So what's it gonna be?"

She backed into the refrigerator; she had nowhere else to go, so she braced her hands at her sides and glared at him. "This is silly. Stop it at once!"

He ignored her command. "Let's see, what shall I claim as my prize? It wasn't a very big or important bet so I'm just looking for a *little* prize, some little something you'll never miss...but which will remind you that nobody gets the best of Garrett Jackson."

He leaned closer. Although he wasn't touching her, she felt his physical presence as if he held her in his arms. Her breathing was erratic, and she couldn't get enough oxygen to think straight.

If she'd been thinking straight, she would never

have said in that faint little voice, "How about a cookie? That's a little something I'll never m-miss."

His smile, she was beginning to realize, was simply glorious when he unfolded it slowly and deliberately, as he did now.

"How about a kiss?" he countered, still not touching her but leaning very near. "Surely that would remind you that I'm a man who likes to win...and does."

And as the final word faded away, he pressed his lips to hers.

CHAPTER THREE

GARRETT pressed his lips against hers...cool and smooth and thrilling. Stiff with shock, she simply stood there as if paralyzed and let him kiss her.

It was the most powerfully erotic kiss she'd ever received, perhaps because there was only that single point of contact between them. He didn't put his arms around her or even lean toward her, although trapped between his body and the refrigerator, she couldn't have retreated any farther if she'd tried.

Her every sense was centered in the growing warmth of his mouth so persuasively controlling hers, the growing warmth of her blood singing through her veins with the sparkle of champagne.

Only slowly did it dawn on her that someone was calling his name. She opened her eyes, unsure when she might have closed them, and blinked, trying to find her bearings.

When she succeeded, she shoved him away and stepped aside, surprised she could stand on legs that trembled this violently. My goodness, that man could kiss! She'd never encountered anything so seductive in her entire life.

But why was *he* frowning? She hadn't put any moves on him! Before she could ask, that unfamiliar female voice intruded again.

"Mr. Jackson? Are you there? Where is everybody? Honestly, if you think I've come all this way to wander around in some *forest*—''

My goodness, Brooke thought groggily, her gaze meeting Garrett's, what a strident voice. It was one he apparently recognized, however, for his look of shock and displeasure was quickly replaced by one closely resembling resignation.

"Mrs. Sisk," he announced with a significant glance at Brooke, as if that were explanation enough.

"Who's Mrs. Sisk?" Brooke found she had trouble using her voice and swallowed hard.

"Molly's nanny." He watched her closely, as if trying to gauge her reaction to his recent sneaky advances. "I forgot all about her."

From the annoyed tone of the woman's voice, Brooke didn't blame him for at least trying. "Nevertheless, I'd say she arrived in the nick of time," she replied tartly. "If you think you can go around stealing kisses any time you feel like it—"

"Hey, that wasn't highway robbery or anything. I won that kiss fair and square." A roguish grin tilted his mouth at one corner. "In fact, *I* was robbed. I didn't get to finish it."

"Oh, yes, you did." Brooke squared her shoulders and pointed toward the door. "You're *really* finished. Now you've got to face the music."

He gave an exaggerated sigh. "Okay, but this only delays the inevitable. Your time will come, Ms. Brooke Hamilton."

Which was exactly what worried her, she admitted, following him into the other room. *Thank you from the bottom of my heart, Mrs. Sisk!*

All gratitude quickly fled, however, for Mrs. Sisk was not the kind of woman who evoked such tender emotion. In fact, Brooke thought, poor Molly had a nanny who looked more like an aging Amazon than a nurturer.

A large woman, she stood beside the sofa where Molly still dozed with Lombard curled up beside her. Fists firmly planted on her hips, the nanny stared down at child and cat with patent disapproval. Dressed in a shapeless gray dress and boxy gray wool jacket, with her jet-black hair pulled back into a bun at the nape of her neck, she looked exactly like somebody's idea of an old maid schoolteacher of a century ago.

"What is the meaning of this?" She indicated the pair on the sofa.

"Uh..." Garrett frowned. "No meaning, beyond the fact that Molly was tired and fell asleep."

"I am talking about *that animal.*"

Lombard glared up at the newcomer with a look of pure feline animosity on her furry face. She did not, however, offer to move.

Brooke rushed in to smooth troubled waters. "*That animal* is just a cat, actually a very sweet cat."

"An oxymoron if I ever heard one." Mrs. Sisk dismissed Brooke with a flick of her stubby eyelashes. "Mr. Jackson, whatever are you thinking of? This practically constitutes child abuse."

Garrett recoiled. "Oh, come on now—"

"Molly's allergic to cats."

"She is?" Garrett looked alarmed. "Really? I had no idea."

Brooke couldn't believe it; he didn't know his own child's allergies? Then an even better question occurred to her. "Are you sure?" she asked. "Molly hasn't sneezed or wheezed or—"

"Young woman, who *are* you?"

"I'm—why, I'm—" Brooke stammered to a halt; why should she feel anxious and defensive before this woman's hostility? She lifted her chin. "I'm Brooke Hamilton and this is my house." She glanced at Lombard. "And that's my cat. In fact, this house is *full* of cats and Molly loves them all."

"In that case," Mrs. Sisk promised in a chilly tone, "we'll make sure she doesn't come here again."

"Oh, dear," Brooke said, "are you another one of those dog people who hate cats?"

"Mrs. Sisk is an equal opportunity animal hater," Garrett intervened. He did not look pleased. "She doesn't like Baron and Larry any more than she likes Lombard."

Mrs. Sisk sniffed. "Animals have their place, I suppose, but it's not inside a civilized house. Molly's mother would not approve." She leaned down to shake the little girl's shoulder. As her hand passed Lombard's head, the white cat hissed and leapt away. Mrs. Sisk jerked her hand back. "He attacked me!"

Garrett stepped forward. "Calm down, Mrs. Sisk. You startled the cat, that's all. I'll carry Molly back to the house for you."

"That won't be necessary." The woman turned that disapproving glance upon him. "If we are to build the child's character, she must learn to do things for herself."

Garrett's expression hardened. "Don't you think that's carrying discipline just a tad too far? After all, she's only a—"

"It was her mother's wish."

Garrett's shoulders slumped almost imperceptibly. "All right." He gave in, but his eyes were narrow and intense. "But don't get too carried away, Mrs. Sisk. She's only a child and I want her to enjoy her summer."

"I will assume responsibility for her summer, Mr. Jackson." The nanny dismissed him by turning away. "Molly, wake up, dear. We have to go now."

And they did, the drowsy child stumbling along without protest beside her stiff-shouldered keeper.

As soon as they were out of sight, Brooke turned on Garrett. "What an awful woman! How can you leave Molly's care to her?"

He looked equally grim. "Mrs. Sisk was Molly's mother's nanny. The woman told the truth—Melinda *did* choose her, and trusted her completely."

Melinda, Molly's mother. Still, Brooke had to try. "Even so, she's very—"

"You don't understand," he interrupted in a tone of sharp annoyance. "She's not usually that abrupt. She's cross because she didn't want to come here for the summer, and because I wasn't at the airport to meet her."

That sounded reasonable, but in any case, it really wasn't any of her business, Brooke reminded herself. "Of course." She gave in. "I shouldn't have said anything."

His sudden smile dazzled her. "In that case, I'll

forgive you." He leaned forward and captured her chin between thumb and forefinger. "I'm pretty ticked with her myself, interrupting payment of our bet that way."

She lifted her chin from his light grip and turned away, although she still felt the burning imprint of his touch. "I told you, I don't bet."

"Everybody bets—on something."

"Not me," she disagreed firmly. "I'm far too cautious to gamble."

"Cautious...or afraid?"

"I'm not—" But she realized instantly that she was afraid: afraid of losing. Coming from a poor, dysfunctional family, she'd had so little in her life that she treasured what was hers, however modest. She might give it away—and often did—but she would not throw it away foolishly.

"Struck a nerve, did I?" He cocked his head, his expression assessing. "I'm a gambler in that I'm willing to take chances—on life, mostly. Nothing ventured, nothing gained."

Easy for him to say, Brooke thought. He came from old money and a prominent family, or so Miss Cora's attorney had said. For Garrett, there was always plenty more where that came from, if his gambles failed to pay off. "Whatever," she said vaguely. "Just don't gamble with your daughter's welfare."

"Agreed. And speaking of my daughter..." He suddenly sounded less glib. "I think there's something you should know about—"

A pounding on the door interrupted him, closely

followed by a woman's voice. "Brooke? Brooke, it's Katy. Can I come in?"

Garrett actually looked relieved. He took a step toward the door. "I'll let her in on my way out," he offered.

"But you were saying something about Molly..."

He waved her query aside. "There'll be plenty of time for that."

She followed him. "Your aunt Cora asked me to help her heirs in any way I can. I should already have begun sorting and cataloging her things but I'm afraid I hadn't gotten around to even starting until today. Then you showed up and—"

He opened the door and Katy almost fell inside. Her freckled face turned up and when she saw him, her jaw dropped.

He grabbed her hand and pumped it. "Glad to meet you..."

"Katy," she supplied, her eyes wide.

"Katy, right. I'm Garrett Jackson. See you around."

"But—" She gaped at him.

"But—" Brooke echoed.

Garrett added to Brooke, "We've got a lot of things to hash out. Why don't you come up to the house for breakfast tomorrow?"

"I...why, I don't—that is—"

"Bet you turn me down." He winked at her, saluted the staring Katy with one hand and walked out of the house.

While seconds ticked by, the two women stood there staring after him, following his progress along the trail through the pines. Then Katy let out her breath on a long, impressed note.

"Wow!" she said softly. "There goes a totally excellent specimen of male pulchritude!"

Brooke responded with a reserved chuckle. "He's...all right, I suppose."

"All right?" Katy followed her hostess through the sitting room and into the kitchen, perfectly at home in her best friend's house. "He's drop-dead gorgeous and you know it." She glanced over her shoulder as if to make sure he wasn't near enough to overhear. "So that's Miss Cora's heir, huh? And he'll be living right next door to you, you lucky thing—yum-yum!"

"For a while, anyway." Brooke scooped ice into two glasses, then reached for the pitcher of lemonade. Uneasily she changed the subject by asking Katy about her boss, Dr. John Harvey, a veterinarian who cared for all the Catty-Corner animals.

Even when confronted with a new and intriguing man, redheaded Katy could be counted on to swoon over Dr. John, as she did now. By concentrating hard, Brooke was able to put Garrett Jackson and his appealing daughter right out of her mind...mostly.

But in the middle of the night, as she tossed and turned in her bed on the second floor, she couldn't help thinking about her handsome new neighbor. Garrett was dangerous to her peace of mind, and so much more. It took a while but by the time she fell asleep, she'd decided upon the proper course of action.

She'd simply pull up the drawbridge, so to speak,

and have as little to do with the Jacksons as possible. It was the only way.

Her new resolve didn't last twelve hours.

Brooke had just finished feeding her "boarders"—breakfast in bed indeed!—when she detected a faint tapping on her front door. Surprised, she answered the summons to find Molly Jackson standing there, wearing matching blue shorts and T-shirt and a furtive expression.

"Why, Molly!" Brooke looked around for Garrett or Mrs. Sisk and saw neither. "What are you doing here so early in the morning, honey?"

"I came to see Lombard," Molly said hopefully. "Can I, please?"

"Sure. Come on in." Brooke guided the girl inside the house. "Are you alone?"

Molly nodded. She was too busy looking around the room to respond verbally. Spotting Lombard on the upholstered and tasseled hassock, she darted forward with a little squeak of pleasure.

Brooke felt her new resolve *dis*solve. You had to love a child who loved your cats, after all. Watching the girl clutch the agreeable white creature to her chest, Brooke sighed. "Sweetheart, does your father or Mrs. Sisk know you've come to visit me?"

"Gart's sleeping," Molly said. "He doesn't like it when I wake him up."

The louse! "Uh...what about your nanny? Does she know? Did you ask her if you could come?"

Molly looked defensive. "She'd say no. She always says no, but I thought you'd say yes." Molly's smile blossomed as suddenly as her father's was prone to do, and Brooke reacted the same way: she melted.

Nevertheless, she couldn't allow this; she must be strong. "I'll have to call the house and tell them you're here," she said firmly. Trying to ignore the girl's crestfallen expression, she started for the telephone. "We wouldn't want anyone to worry—"

"Aha!"

Mrs. Sisk stood on the porch, all righteous indignation. "I knew I'd find you here," she said to Molly, whose shoulders drew together defensively. "As for *you*—"

Brooke's reaction to the woman's attention was the same as Molly's. But being older and arguably wiser, she fought it, squaring her shoulders and facing the nanny. "I beg your pardon?" she said.

Mrs. Sisk opened the screen door and entered. "Young woman, I must ask you—no, I'm *insisting*— that you stop encouraging this child's defiant behavior."

"Oh, really, Mrs. Sisk, I wouldn't call it defiant." All right, she was trying to appease the woman, but it was for Molly's sake. "She just wanted to visit the cats. Surely—"

"How many children have you reared?"

"Well, none—but I was one, once. It wasn't so long ago that I've forgotten."

Mrs. Sisk took Molly's hand. "That attitude is not amusing."

"I'm sorry, I was just trying to get you to lighten up." Brooke gave Molly an encouraging smile. "Kids and pets just seem to go together naturally. You can hardly blame Molly if she—"

"Your views on child rearing do not interest me in the slightest." Leading Molly toward the door, Mrs. Sisk paused. "I must insist that you stop interfering with my attempts to cure this child of the bad habits she's picked up since going to live with *him*."

"Him?" Brooke blinked in bewilderment. "Him, Garrett, her father? She didn't always live with him? Who did she live—"

"That is no concern of yours," the woman cut in. "I'm asking you to please mind your own business. It's for the child's good, I assure you."

Mrs. Sisk hustled Molly away while Brooke stood there with her mouth hanging open in astonishment. The slamming of the door roused her from a state of total shock and she sprang forward, intent upon rescuing the girl.

Garrett met her going out as he was coming out. He caught her hands and whirled her in a circle, his expression cautious.

"Whoa! Hang on there, Brooke."

"But I've got to make that woman understand that—"

"Bad idea."

"You don't know what she said to me, how she was treating that poor little—"

All of a sudden Brooke realized who held her and she drew back. "Garrett! That woman said—"

"Come inside and we'll talk about it."

"But—"

He looked unusually serious, the teasing light gone

from his golden eyes. "Please, Brooke. We need to talk."

His change in attitude got through to her and she stopped struggling, although reluctantly. Was he as insensitive to the plight of his child as he seemed or was there something else going on here? Despite her recent vow to keep her distance, she found herself nodding.

That earned her a brilliant smile. "And maybe you could fix me a little breakfast while we're at it," he added, guiding her back inside with one hand resting lightly at the small of her back.

When she darted him a suspicious glance, he shrugged and raised one eyebrow. "It's not exactly breakfast in bed, but you can't blame a man for taking what he can get."

Oh, couldn't she?

She sat across from him at the work island in the middle of the kitchen, sipping coffee while he dug into a cheese omelet and thick slices of whole wheat toast dripping with homemade peach jam. His blissful expression told her how much he enjoyed her efforts on his behalf.

Not that she'd gone to any extra trouble, she assured herself. A simple omelet was little more trouble than pouring a bowl of cold cereal. She stifled a smile. Who was she kidding? She wouldn't dream of giving this man cold cereal!

He spread more jam. "This is great," he said enthusiastically. "Where'd you learn to cook like this?"

"From one of Miss Cora's chefs, actually."

He looked surprised. "I thought girls learned from their mothers."

"My mother wasn't much of a cook."

"Neither was mine."

That drew a reluctant smile from her. "But with a difference, I suspect. My mother couldn't afford to hire someone to do it for her, so we all got real good with a can opener."

"We?" He licked a speck of jam off his lip, an action brimming with implications.

"I have a sister—wait a minute!" She sat up straighter. "I don't want to talk about me, I want to talk about Molly. And you, for that matter."

"Me?" He looked pleased.

"Don't get any ideas," she ordered primly. "Mrs. Sisk said something I didn't understand."

His raised brows asked the question.

"If Molly's only lived with you for a short time, where did she live before?" Brooke wanted to know.

"I meant to tell you about that." He laid his fork beside an empty plate. "Molly isn't mine. I mean, she's mine now, but I'm not her real father."

She frowned. "I don't understand."

"She's my older brother Brock's child. He and his wife died in a terrible car accident about eight months ago. They left custody of their only child to me."

"Oh, Garrett!" Her heart went out to him and to the little girl who'd been so cruelly orphaned. "You didn't know they were going to do that?"

"Actually, I did." Using both hands, he brushed dark hair away from his face in an anxious gesture unlike any she'd seen him make before. "When they came to me and explained their reasoning right after she was born, I said, 'Sure, why not?' I mean, there really wasn't anyone else, and I never dreamed for a minute that anything would happen to them.''

"I'm sure it must have been an awful shock," she whispered.

"And then some. They were much too young to die, and God knows Molly was much too young to lose both her parents like that."

"At least she had you," she reminded him.

His laugh sounded skeptical. "Such as I was, the scandal of Chicago. All their friends thought they were crazy to choose me, since I'd been leading a somewhat...profligate life." He darted her a veiled glance as if to see whether or not she could read between the lines.

"Playboy of the western world, I suppose," she interpreted lightly.

"Something like that," he admitted. "But with my new responsibilities, I've tried to turn myself around and get serious. Suddenly there's more at stake than just me."

"So that's why Molly calls you Gart," Brooke mused aloud.

He nodded. "She used to call me *Uncle* Gart. It really confused her the first time someone referred to me as her daddy. She knows her daddy is dead. She's not about to let anyone take his place, so now she just calls me Gart, without the uncle. I'm ready for anything she's comfortable with."

"But you'd like it if she called you daddy," Brooke guessed.

He sighed. "If wishes were horses— Anyway, that's why I may sometimes seem uncertain where Molly's concerned. I haven't had a whole lot of practice yet at this father stuff."

"Thank you for telling me. It's easier to understand, now." She thought for a moment. "You had nothing to do with choosing Mrs. Sisk, then."

He rolled his eyes. "Do I look crazy or something?"

"But you won't fire her because she was Molly's mother's choice."

"That's right." He leaned forward in appeal. "She's not so bad, honest. She's got tons of experience and Melinda thought she was wonderful. I'll admit, she's not a warm person—"

Brooke inserted a dubious exclamation.

"But I feel as if I'm stuck with her."

"What would you do if she got mad and quit?"

"Throw a party? Dance a jig? Call out for pizza?"

She nodded emphatically. "Then get ready, because I don't think she'll last the summer here."

"*I* may not last the summer here."

She'd forgotten about that; she'd *tried* to forget about that. "Then you really meant what you said about selling Miss Cora's bequest?" she ventured, against her better judgment.

"Of course." He drained his coffee cup. "Any more of that stuff in the pot?"

"No!" She stood up, all her kind feelings toward him flying out the window. "I think you'd better go now."

"Ah, Brooke, don't be like that. This is the real

world. What would I want with that big old tomb on
the hill? I've lived my entire life in Chicago and that's
where I belong. Of course, I'm going to sell it.''

''But Miss Cora's will—''

''Wills can be broken.''

''To some people,'' she whispered, ''*anything* can
be broken.''

He didn't look offended. ''And everything has its
price,'' he said.

She shook her head violently. ''Not everything.''

''Yes, everything.'' Leaning forward, he covered
her hand with his and held it when she tried to with-
draw. ''Brooke, I intend to buy your land and this
house.''

''Never!''

''I'll pay you handsomely.''

''You won't pay me at all because I'm not selling,
not now and not ever.''

''You will.''

''How do you expect to make me? Waving money
at me won't do it.''

''Maybe, maybe not.''

She quivered like a tuning fork, all her senses centered in her hand beneath his. ''We were talking about
Mrs. Sisk,'' she reminded him desperately. ''She
doesn't like me or my cats or, I strongly suspect, Colorado—perhaps everything west of the
Mississippi. Neither Colorado nor I are likely to
change so you'd better be prepared for her to leave
you in the lurch.'' Which would be the best thing that
could possibly happen to Molly, she thought.

He measured her with a long glance. "Want to bet?" he challenged.

"No, I do not want to bet!"

"If she walks, I'll serve you breakfast in bed. If she sticks out the summer, you'll serve me—"

"Hemlock!" But she couldn't help laughing at the hopeful expression on his face. "Honestly, Garrett, you've got a one-track mind."

He grinned back. "So I've been told. Is it a bet, then?"

"It certainly is not. I told you, I'm not a betting woman. I don't take silly chances."

"Silly chances?" he interrupted quickly. "What kind of chance are we talking about here, unless you get nervous putting me in the same sentence with *bed*."

"You're incredibly conceited, did you know that?"

"I'm incredibly realistic." He leaned over the work counter until his face was very near hers. "Sometimes I'm incredibly fatalistic...like now."

"I...I don't know what you mean," she said primly—but she did. She did so well....

"I mean that I find you extremely attractive."

She leaned away from him, her breath coming more quickly. "Maybe you think it's fun to tease me but it's not very nice," she scolded him.

"Tease you? I'm not teasing." He picked up her hand and brushed his lips across her knuckles. "Hey, it's going to be a long, hot summer—"

"Not in Colorado, it isn't. We keep our cool here."

That sexy smile curved his mobile mouth. "Time will tell, Ms. Hamilton. Time will tell—but I'm putting my money on a long, hot summer. We might as well make the most of it, don't you think?''

"I certainly do not." She lifted her chin. "If you're looking for a summer fling, you're looking in the wrong place."

"Hey, I didn't pick the location, my aunt Cora did." He released her hand and stood up. "Will you come up to the house this afternoon and help me start going through all that stuff?"

"Of course." She had to do it; she couldn't let Miss Cora down.

"And maybe tomorrow you can show me Boulder," he suggested.

"That's not part of the deal."

"Okay, let's make it part of a *bet*. If I win, you show me Boulder. If you win, you show me Boulder. That makes it a win-win proposition. So what'll we bet on?"

She couldn't help laughing. "I won't bet and that's final."

Just then Gable strolled through the kitchen door, crossed the slate tiles and twined himself around Garrett's ankles. Garret gave her a pained glance. "Why don't we bet on whether the cats or the dogs screw up first?"

"My cats do not screw up."

"Then you have nothing to worry about." He gave her a graceful salute with one hand. "See you after lunch, all right?"

It wasn't a bit all right, but she couldn't think of a convincing way to tell him that before he'd walked away.

CHAPTER FOUR

OF COURSE, Brooke went. She couldn't stay away when the subject was Glennhaven. Passing through the wrought-iron gates and walking around to the front of the stately stone mansion, she looked up at it with fresh appreciation.

The three-story house with its generous turret had been built by an eccentric scientist in 1895 on this mountainside west of Boulder. It had seventeen rooms and a multitude of amenities added over the years by its various owners, including a glass-enclosed swimming pool installed by Miss Cora herself.

"When I came here from California in 1934," she used to say, "everybody who was anybody had a swimming pool—even if they lived in the snow zone!"

Could Garrett really intend to sell this jewel? Brooke idly stroked Gable, draped over her shoulder like an old-fashioned fur stole. If he did, he'd be selling his own family's history. With fresh determination to thwart such an atrocity, she lifted the gleaming brass knocker and let it fall with a solid *thump*.

Garrett himself answered the summons, to her great relief. She wasn't sure how she'd have responded had the overwhelming Mrs. Sisk stood there. Actually, looking at the tall, handsome man before her, she realized she wasn't sure how to respond to *him*, either.

From the first moment she'd seen him, she'd found herself strangely rattled in his presence. This occasion proved to be no exception.

With a dubious glance at the cat on her shoulder, he gestured her inside. "I need you," he said plaintively. "We've poked around a bit, but we keep getting lost. This place is a rabbit warren."

She glared at him. "It certainly is not! It's a fabulous historic treasure trove." She glanced around with a frown. "Where's Molly?"

"With Mrs. Sisk. Shall we get started?"

Just the two of them? She'd counted on Molly's distracting presence. A twinge of panic flared in her chest but there was nothing for her to do but agree.

Slowly she led him through the rooms of Glennhaven, pointing out details in which she soon became engrossed: the stained-glass windows, the bird's-eye maple moldings and doors, priceless Oriental carpets on the floors and equally priceless original paintings on the walls.

And everywhere, photographs, many fading and sepia-toned, most of Miss Cora: as an angelic child who looked a bit like Molly, as a fresh young girl facing the future with boundless optimism, as a teenage beauty just entering films, and finally, as a mature woman of heart-stopping glamour and unparalleled mystique.

Garrett paused in the first-floor library with its mirror-polished cherrywood tables and bookshelves. Picking up a photograph in an ornate Art Deco frame, he stared intently at the picture of his late great-aunt.

"I had no idea she was so beautiful," he said in a tone of surprise.

"Surely you've seen other photos of her," Brooke suggested.

He shook his head. "Not really. There were no pictures of her that I know of in our family. No one ever spoke of her."

"But her films—"

He shook his head again. "I'm not really a movie fan anyway, but those old silent films? I'd never be able to sit through one of them."

"I'll bet you could." The unintended word—*bet*— just slipped out. She added hastily, "That is—"

His laughter stopped her. "There's a bet I can't possibly lose."

She gave him a sheepish smile. "That's not what I meant and you know it. I just mean that silent films are really quite fascinating, especially Miss Cora's. She had quite a film library."

"Perhaps someday you'll show me your favorite."

"I'll be happy to make recommendations," she said primly.

His heavy-lidded gaze warmed her. "I said, *show* me. I'll buy the popcorn."

Sit in a darkened room with him, alone in the shared intimacy of a romantic old movie? "We'll see," she hedged, but what she really meant was *no way*! "Now, over here," she directed, "you'll notice the workmanship on this fireplace. There are nine fireplaces in the house and each one is different. This one has an intricate design of carved wood...."

As she explained, she pointed out details with loving attention. Subject successfully changed, she led him next into the kitchen. She paused next to the marble counter designed for rolling pastry to be baked in the huge coal-burning stove.

"Who's doing the cooking for you, by the way?" she inquired.

He made a face. "Mrs. Sisk, with reluctance, until I can hire someone."

She trailed a fingertip over the cool marble surface with its delicate blue veining. "You don't cook?"

He took a step back, his face a study in astonishment. "Do I really look like the kind of man who'd know his way around a kitchen?" He sounded insulted she might think so.

"Well..." She gave him an oblique glance. "The way you keep bringing up breakfast in bed, I naturally assumed you'd be prepared to pay off."

Leaning forward, he touched her chin with his fingertips, turning her face so he could look into her eyes. "I don't intend to lose," he murmured. "But if I should, by some fluke...I'll be prepared to pay up, in style. You can count on it."

She took a hasty step away, breaking that mesmerizing contact. Each time he touched her, she found herself trembling and distracted. "Good luck finding a cook, then," she said. "Now, about this marble slab— It was installed as part of the original house when it was built in 1895."

He frowned down at the gleaming surface with its smooth indentations created by decades of dedicated cooks. "What's it for?"

"Rolling pastry, making candy, that sort of thing.

The marble remains cool no matter what the weather, which is a great help to the cook.''

He looked doubtful. "Kind of old-fashioned. And that stove—" He indicated the huge, old, coal-burning cooking stove against one wall. "What was she, stuck in the past?"

"Not at all." Brooke tried to control her resentment at the mere suggestion. "Miss Cora was a thoroughly modern woman." Swinging open a series of folding doors, she revealed a complete modern cooking center with microwave and conventional ovens. "She kept the old stove because she appreciated its history, not because she longed for the olden days."

Garrett cocked his head thoughtfully. "I'm beginning to suspect she must have been quite a complicated old lady."

"She was that, and a whole lot more." Brooke felt a sudden rush of nostalgia, a longing for days gone by that Miss Cora herself probably wouldn't even have understood. "This place hasn't been the same without her," she admitted after a moment.

"Another good reason to dispose of it," he inserted smoothly. "What's through that door?"

Shocked, she led him on through the dining room with crystal, china and linens on display; the morning room with its sunny yellow decor; and finally into the Great Room, which soared two stories high.

He tilted back his head to stare up at the ornamented ceiling. "Good Lord," he said. "What is this, the Sistine Chapel?"

Brooke laughed uneasily. "Miss Cora actually used this room for parties in the early days, but by the time

I came here, she was a widow and it was pretty much ignored. A shame, too. It's a beautiful room and she—''

A telephone rang in the hall. With a shrug, he went to answer.

Lingering just inside the door, Brooke eavesdropped shamelessly on the one-sided conversation.

"Oh, hi, Dee-Dee... Yeah, we made it fine... I'm sorry, that's impossible. Honey, I told you I'd be gone all summer... Yeah, yeah, I miss you, too. Uh-huh. Sure. Right. Later.''

By the time he reentered the room, Brooke was deep in consideration of one of the many magnificent light fixtures. But her thoughts were on the unknown Dee-Dee. Garrett Jackson really was a ladies' man. She must never lose sight of that fact.

"Sorry about the interruption,'' he said. "Shall we go on?''

So they did. She led him to the second floor with its billiard room, gentlemen's room, ladies' powder room, music room, and into a carefully lighted art gallery featuring the work of some of the world's most renowned artists. Her heart wasn't in it, though. She kept thinking about his conversation with the woman named Dee-Dee. No wonder he was such an accomplished flirt, she thought indignantly. He was obviously getting plenty of practice.

He leaned close to a landscape oil in a carefully lighted alcove, examining the signature. "Good copy,'' he announced.

Brooke sniffed indignantly. "Good original.'' She turned away. "As you already know, the bedrooms are on the third floor. The pool and tennis courts are out back, as are the stables.''

He looked alarmed. ''That big building is a stable? Don't tell me I'm going to have to contend with a herd of horses on top of everything else.''

That brought a smile, which cleared away some of her tension. ''No horses. At least, since I've been here, the building's been used for storage. But when this house was constructed, horses and carriages were a necessity. The other building is a kennel—''

As if on cue, Garrett's German shepherd wandered into the room. Familiar panic gripped Brooke's chest in a vise. The dog saw his master and approached with lazily wagging tail, but still Brooke shrank away. Automatically she clutched at the cat still draped across her shoulder.

Garrett gave Brooke a curious glance. ''You don't have to be afraid of old Baron,'' he assured her. ''He wouldn't harm a fly.''

Chewing on her lower lip and never taking her gaze off the dog, Brooke edged toward the door. ''I'll take your word for it,'' she said, not meaning it at all.

''No, really—''

Mrs. Sisk sailed into the room. ''Mr. Jackson, a woman is here to apply for the position of cook. I've already spoken to her at length and am prepared to tell you that she simply won't do.'' Her gaze zeroed in on Gable. ''What is that creature doing in this house?''

Brooke felt the orange cat tense, his claws digging delicately into her T-shirt. ''This house is the only home Gable ever knew until Miss Cora's death,'' she explained, trying not to upset the woman any more but determined to defend the cat's territorial rights. "He always comes along with me when I'm here."

"I see." If so, she obviously didn't like it. She returned her attention to Garrett. "About that cook, Mr. Jackson—"

"What's her name?" Brooke asked. "Perhaps I know her."

Mrs. Sisk didn't look as if that would be much of a recommendation. At Garrett's nod, she tightened her lips in disapproval before finally answering. "Her name is O'Hara, I believe she said."

"Mary O'Hara?" Brooke glanced at Garrett. "Mary O'Hara's worked here before."

"So she told me repeatedly." Mrs. Sisk did not look impressed.

Brooke kept her tone pleasant but it wasn't easy. "Mrs. O'Hara left because her youngest daughter was having a baby and needed her. Miss Cora always hoped she'd come back someday."

"Is that so," Mrs. Sisk sounded disinterested. "Nevertheless, she is not at all suitable."

Garrett, who had been watching the two women with a calculating expression in his golden eyes, took over. "Why isn't she suitable, Mrs. Sisk?"

The nanny cast Brooke a guarded glance. "Because she took one look at Molly and announced that gingerbread cookies were her specialty." The tone of the woman's voice declared such a skill worthless.

"I like gingerbread cookies," Garrett said ominously.

Mrs. Sisk squared her already-square shoulders. "I hardly think that is a proper recommendation for—"

"What you think about the people I hire is beside the point, Mrs. Sisk."

At his quiet but powerful declaration, the woman looked shocked. "But, Mr. Jackson!"

He waved her protests aside. "I'll speak to Mrs. O'Hara and *I'll* decide whether or not she is suitable. Your only responsibility here is Molly's health and happiness. I suggest you see to that now."

"Well, I never!"

Whirling, the woman stalked from the room. Garrett looked thoughtful but when he turned toward Brooke, it was with a pleasant smile. "Shall we go speak to Mrs. O'Hara?" he asked, his tone as even as though the disagreeable scene had never taken place.

She nodded and led the way downstairs, being careful to stay as far away from the dog as possible. Her thoughts, however, were on the man, not the animal.

What a complicated person Garrett Jackson was...a lot like his great-aunt in that respect.

Mrs. O'Hara greeted them with a smile. A plump, grandmotherly woman in her late fifties or early sixties, she'd be the perfect counterbalance to the prickly Mrs. Sisk, Brooke thought, introducing her to Garrett.

Mrs. O'Hara stuck out her hand and pumped his. "I met that little daughter of yours," she declared with enthusiasm which rang with sincerity. "She's a perfect angel. I'd enjoy cookin' for her, I must say."

Garrett grinned at her. "You're hired."

The woman blinked in surprise. "Just like that? Don't you want to check my references and so forth and so on?"

"Your references are impeccable," he assured her, glancing at Brooke. "Ms. Hamilton speaks very highly of you."

Mrs. O'Hara beamed. "I speak very highly of her, too. How have you been, Brooke, dear?"

"Just fine, Mrs. O'Hara."

"But you're missin' Miss Cora, I'll bet."

Brooke's smile felt misty. "That's a bet you'd win. I do miss her, terribly."

"But now this young man is here to take the reins so things'll be just fine again," the woman predicted briskly, rubbing her hands together. "When do you want me to start, Mr. Jackson? Now?" She looked around the room with an expression of anticipation. "I've missed this old place and I'm mighty glad to be comin' back."

"Tomorrow will do just fine," Garrett assured her. "We're pleased to have you with us, Mrs. O'Hara."

"And I'm pleased—"

Something black and white streaked into the room and Mrs. O'Hara gave a little shriek of alarm. It was Larry, skidding to a sitting halt in the midst of the circle of three. He looked up at the new cook, panting, his tongue lolling out of the side of his mouth. He almost seemed to be smiling at her.

Mrs. O'Hara leaned down to pat his furry head. "My goodness," she exclaimed. "I hope Miss Cora's not turning over in her grave with a dog in her house!"

"Dogs plural," Brooke corrected, wondering why in the world an otherwise intelligent woman would get friendly with a strange dog. She felt Gable shifting on her shoulder and didn't blame him one bit for being uneasy in the presence of that obnoxious little animal. "Actually, there are two of them. The other's a German shep—"

She didn't have a chance to finish her explanation before Gable launched himself at the furry four-footed intruder like a dog-seeking missile.

Garrett had been waiting for that damned cat to screw up but when the time came, it caught him as much by surprise as it did the others. The blasted animal landed with all four feet on poor old Larry's back. For a minute there, the air was filled with flying feet and claws and teeth, not to mention terrible snarls and panic-filled yelps.

Then as quickly as it began, the battle was over and the big orange cat looked down from a safe perch high atop a kitchen cabinet. Old dumb Larry all but chased his tail in frustration, apparently lacking a clue as to where his foe had fled.

And damn if the cat didn't look full of satisfaction at the way he'd pulled off that sneak attack. Garrett burst out laughing; he couldn't help himself, even knowing Brooke would turn on him in outrage.

Which she did. "How can you laugh at a time like this?" she demanded. "That horrible dog could have killed Miss Cora's poor cat!"

She was adorable in her fury, her trim little body unyielding in khaki shorts and a white blouse tucked in primly at the waistband. He had a sudden impulse to take her in his arms and kiss her until she forgot all about the stupid cat.

Mrs. O'Hara fanned her flushed face with one hand. "Goodness, that was close," she exclaimed. "Do they do that often?"

Brooke's glare didn't soften. "You mean, does that horrible dog try to kill my cats often?"

Garrett shook his head in feigned disbelief. "That's twice you've unjustly accused old Larry of starting a fight," he said. "You need to teach your cat some manners, Brooke."

"My cat has perfect manners!"

"He launched a completely unprovoked sneak attack on Molly's dog."

"A good offense is the best defense," she retorted.

"Call it what you will, it's definitely lost the bet for you."

"What bet?" asked Mrs. O'Hara, who'd been watching the exchange with interest gleaming in her blue eyes.

"There's no bet," Brooke said quickly, her expression alternately ordering and begging Garrett not to pursue this line of conversation.

He ignored both. "We had a bet as to whether her cats or my dogs would screw up first," he informed the cook. "I'm clearly the winner."

"I didn't accept the bet!" Brooke wailed. She walked to the cabinet and reached toward the cat, who sat looking at the scene below with unblinking yellow eyes. She cast a frustrated glance at Garrett. "Will you get that dog out of here so I can lure my cat down?''

"Say please," Garrett instructed, struggling to keep a straight face. Damn, he enjoyed teasing her. He wondered why....

A bright blush swept into her cheeks. "Please," she added in a choked little voice.

"Your wish is my command." Leaning down, he scooped up the still-confused Larry, carried him to the door, tossed him outside and closed the door behind him.

Mrs. O'Hara retrieved her big black purse lying on a counter. "So what did you two kids bet?" she inquired without the least bit of reserve.

"Nothing!" Brooke declared. "Gable, you come down here this minute, you naughty cat!"

"We...weren't very specific." Garrett drew it out to annoy Brooke. "But since I won, I guess I get to name my prize."

"No, you don't." Brooke cast him a narrow-eyed glare, then set about dragging a step stool over to the cabinet so she could climb up to retrieve the cat.

"Yes I do." He gave her a nefarious grin. "I choose...breakfast in—"

"Forget it."

"Boulder. Tomorrow morning, with Molly and me. And then you can show us the town."

She had the cat now. She turned on the top step of the stool, her expression startled. Her gleaming brown hair swung smoothly around her cheeks, and her brown eyes sparkled with what looked like confusion. "Oh. I—maybe—" She sighed and gave in. "Okay.

I mean, I guess that would be all right, if it would get you off this kick you're on to turn everything into a bet.''

"Not a chance." Stepping forward, he put his hands on her waist. It was almost as if he could feel the pulse of her body thrumming even there. Damn, she'd make a perfect armful....

"Garrett!''

Her tone warned him, and so did Gable's narrowed eyes; what was the big orange tom, a watch-cat?

"Just doing my gentlemanly duty," he said lightly, swinging her off the stool and onto the floor. He hated to release her, but did anyway. "Tomorrow morning at nine, then. Is that okay?''

She stood where he'd planted her, very close but with the cat clutched to her chest like a shield. Her luminous brown eyes met his as if trying to fathom his true intent, which was impossible to do since his agenda was slowly changing.

He'd come here in large part to find out how this little interloper had manipulated a dotty old woman into leaving her a valuable chunk of property. Now he'd come to realize that Brooke Hamilton didn't have a manipulative bone in her entire body.

That still left him with the problem of convincing her to sell, but in the meantime he was not averse to enlivening a long, hot...*dull*...summer.

At last she sighed. Pulling her gaze away, she murmured, "Okay...I guess.''

Exactly as he'd known she'd do.

Molly and Garrett appeared at Brooke's front door the next morning promptly at nine o'clock. Looking at the two of them, all bright and shining and beautiful, Brooke felt her resistance melting away like Colorado snow in June sunshine.

"Ready to go?" he asked, cocking his head in that quizzical way he had. He wore navy shorts and a yellow T-shirt with white leather sneakers. Freshly shaven, his hair was still damp from his morning shower. In short, he looked absolutely wonderful.

Brooke swallowed hard. "I guess so," she conceded, turning her attention to Molly. "I'm happy to see you again, sweetheart."

"Can I visit the cats, Ms. Brooke?" The little girl looked up with pleading eyes. "Can I hold Lombard? Can I—"

Garrett touched her shoulder lightly. "We're on our way to breakfast," he reminded her gently. "Aren't you hungry, honey?"

She shook her blond hair vigorously. "I'd rather play with the cats. Can I, please?"

He glanced at Brooke as if for acquiescence, which she quickly gave with the faintest of nods. "When we get back, then," he promised. "If it's all right with Brooke—"

"Of course," she agreed quickly. "But right now, I'm starving! If it's all right with you, Garrett, I thought we could go to this wonderful little café on the Pearl Street Mall...."

Boulder's Pearl Street Mall was the heart and center of the city, not to mention a favorite destination for Brooke on her trips into town. The four-block, open-air pedestrian mall was also a proven hit with visitors, and she'd served as tour guide for Miss Cora's friends on any number of occasions.

It was the perfect and obvious spot to take the Jacksons for breakfast, since it afforded Brooke an opportunity to fall into her tour-guide persona. This she did with ease. Directing Garrett down the mountainside to Canyon Boulevard, she pointed out the sights along the way: the doe with her fawn almost hidden by the slender trunks of aspens, the goslings paddling behind their parents on a quiet woodland pond, the first tentative blue blooms of the Colorado columbine.

"The Colorado blue columbine was chosen as the state flower in 1899," Brooke explained to Molly, who was in the back seat.

"Why?" the little girl asked, all big eyes.

Brooke, well prepared to answer that question, smiled. "The blue color is for Colorado's blue skies," she said. "The white petals in the middle are for the snow, and the golden center is for the metal which started the big gold rush in 1859."

"What metal?" Molly asked, triggering laughter from her father.

"Gold, Molly!"

"Oh," she said, sounding disappointed. "I like the baby deer best."

But they were not to see much more in the way of wildlife, for they were approaching the city of Boulder itself, snuggled at the foot of the pine-covered foothills. Brooke slipped once more into her tour-guide mode.

"The population of Boulder is a bit more than ninety thousand," she told Garrett. "But C.U. accounts for better than a quarter of it—that's Colorado University at Boulder."

Garrett slowed the car for they were encountering more traffic. "I had a friend who went to school there," he said. "Good party school, I hear."

"It's a good school period," Brooke said loftily.

He glanced at her, his face filled with curiosity. "Did you go there?"

"Me?" She laughed incredulously. "Not hardly. I couldn't begin to afford it." She leaned forward. "Turn left at the next corner, okay?"

He did, and from that point on most of their mutual attention was given over to navigating the increasingly congested streets. As usual, there seemed to be nearly as many bicycles as cars, and as many runners as bicyclists as they neared the heart of town, traveling past stately old Victorians on their way.

Suddenly Brooke spotted an empty parking space. "Quick, grab it!" she instructed Garrett.

He reacted with equal speed, maneuvering the BMW into the small space with ease. Extracting the key from the ignition, he twisted toward Brooke with a challenging expression.

"Time for breakfast." He drew it out endlessly. "But unfortunately, not in—"

"Garrett!" Brooke shot a meaningful glance toward the back seat.

One corner of his mouth edged up. "Breakfast...in Boulder. Half a loaf is better than none." He pivoted in his bucket seat. "Right, Molly?"

''Uh-huh, Gart.'' But she obviously had no idea what he was talking about, for she added, ''Do I have to eat bread? I want pancakes!''

''So do I,'' Brooke agreed. ''What about you, Garrett? You'll join us in ordering pancakes, won't you?''

''I have something else in mind,'' he declined. ''Would you care to discuss—''

She certainly wouldn't, and put an end to that line of conversation by opening the door and climbing out for the short walk to the mall itself.

CHAPTER FIVE

THE Pearl Street Mall was Boulder's premiere location for people-watching. Travelers came from all over the world to enjoy its ambience. Historic brick and sandstone buildings lined the four-block, open-air pedestrian mall, home to shops and galleries, offices and innumerable sidewalk cafés. Year-round, night and day, the mall provided a stage for a host of interesting characters who came from far and wide to strut their stuff.

At Garrett's urging, Brooke selected one of her favorite eating places, a small café which was one of the few remaining mom 'n' pop operations.

Choosing a table beneath the shade of a striped awning, they made themselves comfortable and were soon enjoying steaming cups of almond-flavored coffee for the adults and orange juice for all. They anxiously awaited the arrival of their selections from the eclectic menu: pancakes and fresh fruit for Brooke and Molly, a breakfast skillet made up of potatoes, eggs and sausage for Garrett.

After a moment spent contemplating tourists strolling through leafy shade, Garrett leaned back in his chair with a sigh of satisfaction. She gave him an anxious glance and he returned a reassuring smile.

She wore a dress today, which she rarely did. A light summer thing, it fell around her slender body in graceful folds, unassuming but flattering. He liked the pretty pink-and-blue print.

"Nice," he said wholeheartedly.

"Pardon me?"

"The scenery," he said, but meaning much more. "Do you come here often?"

She didn't look at him, instead seeming to concentrate on a couple strolling past arm in arm. He didn't believe her lack of attentiveness for a moment but was willing to play along.

"No," she said at last. "Not often. I only come down from the mountain when I have to."

"Have to?" He urged her to continue.

"I like it better at home," she said. "You know, the solitude, the beauty...."

"I see." What he saw was that it would be harder to get her to come around to his point of view than he'd expected. Not impossible, of course; simply harder. Sympathy might do the trick. "I'd think you'd get lonesome way up there, especially now that you're all alone," he ventured.

She blinked as if surprised. "I'm not alone."

Was she referring to him? He lifted in brows in expectation.

"I have my cats," she added quickly, as if she knew what he'd been thinking.

That elicited a good-natured groan from him. "Come on, Brooke. You're a young, beautiful woman—" He stuck in the "beautiful" not only because it was true but because he wanted to gauge her reaction. He wasn't disappointed, for crimson flooded her cheeks and she shifted uncomfortably in her chair.

He went on. "And you must have some kind of social life."

She pursed her lips. "Must I?"

He grinned. "It's a law of nature. You know—boy, girl—"

She tossed back that shiny swing of hair. "If that's true, where's yours?"

"My what?"

"Your girl!" She gave him an impertinent glance.

Amused, he countered in the same light tone. "Is that your not-so-subtle way of finding out if there's a girl-I-left-behind-me?"

"I did hear you talking to a woman on the phone," she admitted.

"You mean Caroline? She's just a friend."

"Who's Caroline? I meant Dee-Dee."

"Oops." He gave her a deliberately charming smile. "Dee-Dee's just a friend, too. I'm a friendly sort of guy."

Brooke didn't look as if she doubted that for a minute. Instead of replying, she turned toward Molly. "You haven't said much, honey. How do you like the mall?"

Molly set her empty orange juice glass back on the table. "It's okay."

"Just okay?" Brooke patted the little girl's cheek with a gentle hand. "What's the matter? Are you bored?"

"Yes," Molly said in a clear, unselfconscious tone.

"Would you like to tell me about it?"

Molly considered for a moment and Garrett found

himself holding his breath. If she'd only talk, even if it weren't to him— But such was not to be.

"No," Molly said with a sigh. "I want to go watch those kids play." She indicated a half dozen or so youngsters clambering over a two-foot-high bronze frog in the middle of the brick-paved mall. Nearby was a rabbit, and further down the mall, a snail and a beaver, all just begging for a kid's attention.

Garrett felt a flash of alarm, as he always did when there was a chance Molly would be beyond his immediate protection. "I don't think that's a good idea," he said uneasily.

"Please, Gart?" She turned pleading eyes on him.

Torn, he hesitated, glancing at Brooke for her two cents worth. He saw both understanding and compassion on her face.

She leaned forward, looking directly at him. "It'll be all right," she assured him. "We can see her the entire time."

"I'm not sure—"

"Please, Gart? Please?"

"Please?" Brooke echoed with a mischievous smile on her face.

He gave her a sheepish smile. "I'm being overprotective, huh?"

"Maybe just a tad." She added hastily, "But it's entirely understandable."

"In that case…" He grimaced. "Okay, Molly, but can you wait until after we eat? Then if you still want to…" Which he hoped she wouldn't.

A flash of disappointment crossed the little girl's face and for a moment she looked as if she might protest. Garrett almost hoped she would. She was too docile, too...too perfect. He'd almost welcome a show of spirit.

He didn't get it. Molly simply sighed and nodded and resumed her hungry perusal of the noisy, happy children.

Their food arrived before he had a chance to reconsider. Presented with a flourish, it tasted as good as it looked and they all ate heartily, even Molly who often only picked at her food. Finishing before the two adults were even well begun, she turned a hopeful face toward Garrett.

"Did I eat good?" she asked anxiously.

He made a great show of examining her plate. She'd consumed half a pancake and nearly all her fresh fruit, a large meal for one so small. "You ate very well indeed," he assured her with a smile.

"Then can I—may I go play with those kids?" She jerked her head toward the children still clambering around on the bronze frog.

He had no choice but to grant permission, which he did with a reluctant nod. "But stay right there where I can see you," he warned. "Okay?"

She leapt to her feet. "Okay!"

Her interest wasn't in him, however; it was locked onto the children and the frog. Her delight almost neutralized his concern. He watched her skip away with mixed emotions.

Brooke looked sympathetic. "It'll be all right, Garrett. She won't be out of our sight for a minute."

"You're right, of course." Somehow he'd lost interest in his breakfast. He put down his fork. "If I seem overprotective..." He wasn't sure where he'd meant to go with this so he let his words trail off. He hoped he didn't sound defensive.

"I wouldn't say that." She reached for a grape. "You're still new at this father business. I think you're doing a wonderful job."

"You do?" He stared at her, surprised and gratified. Accustomed to criticism about his lack of parenting skills from his own circle of acquaintances, he felt a glow of pleasure from her unexpected and unsolicited praise.

She nodded emphatically. He'd noticed that she did most everything emphatically, as if she felt things strongly and wasn't afraid to take a stand.

"It couldn't have been easy," she went on, "a single man taking on such a heavy responsibility. It must have turned your life upside down."

She'd never know how much. "I'd do it again in a heartbeat," he said, meaning it.

She'd been looking everywhere but at him. Now she suddenly lifted her face and met his steady gaze. "Have you ever been married?"

He found her seriousness amusing. "No. You?"

"Of course not."

He couldn't imagine how he might have offended her. "What'd I say?" he asked plaintively.

She relaxed her stiff expression, even managed a slightly sheepish smile. "If I'd ever been married, I'd still be married—or a widow, heaven forbid."

He simply couldn't resist teasing her. "What do I have here, an old-fashioned girl?"

She lifted her small chin. "I can't help it. I just

happen to feel that marriage is forever.'' She cocked her head, giving her an utterly charming smile. ''Could it be that you agree with me? I mean, here you are, thirty...'' She raised her brows in question.

''Two,'' he supplied. ''I'm thirty-two.''

''Old enough to be married and divorced a time or two, if you took marriage lightly.''

''Or,'' he countered, ''maybe I give marriage so little weight that I don't want to be bothered—ever.''

That shocked her; he saw it in the way her beautiful brown eyes widened in what looked like disbelief. But she didn't argue her point. He was more than willing to defend himself if she did, but once again she surprised him.

''That would be incredibly sad, if it were true,'' she said at last. ''Not that it matters to me, of course. Your love life is none of my business.''

''I'd be glad to make it your business.'' Damn, he shouldn't have said that, but the opening was too wide, his interest in her too obvious—at least, to him.

She actually flinched. ''Are you suggesting a summer romance? I don't think so, Mr. Jackson.'' Her tone was as distant as her expression.

''Surely you'd thought of that possibility, Ms. Hamilton,'' he suggested with a crocodile smile.

''Certainly not!'' She looked so flustered that he knew she was lying. ''I was thinking of Molly, that's all. I couldn't possibly be less interested in your love life *or* your marital status. I'm only thinking of Molly.''

''Really? I'm sorry to hear that.'' But not convinced, and not in the least deterred. ''We might have found…ways to make the summer pass rather pleasantly.''

She jumped to her feet, and he saw her hands clench into small fists at her sides. He found himself thinking that she was adorable in her outrage.

"Molly's waving to us," she said abruptly. "If you're finished…''

"Not nearly," he said cryptically, but he, too, stood up. There was no reason to put her on her guard. "Shall we see what's on her mind—and try to ignore what's on ours?''

She opened her mouth to retort, instead groaned and pressed her lips together before turning away. Well satisfied with the exchange, he tossed a handful of bills on the table and followed her out onto the mall.

The drive back up the mountain gave her time to think, and what she thought did not bring her pleasure. Garrett Jackson was a playboy, a love 'em and leave 'em type if she'd ever met one. Usually that type didn't appeal to her in the slightest, but her reaction to her new, if temporary, neighbor was distinctly out of the ordinary.

Stealing a glance at him while he piloted the sleek automobile around a curve, she admired his strong profile. He seemed determined to present himself as some sort of shallow playboy, but she sensed so much more beneath that deceptive surface.

But was that "something more" better or worse than the face he presented to the world? If she had a lick of sense, she wouldn't pursue this line of thought for another minute.

Back at the estate, he pulled the car into her driveway and stopped. Before either adult could say anything, Molly leaned forward.

"Can I come in and visit the cats?" she asked in an anxious little voice. "Please, Gart, can I?"

He tipped his head toward Brooke. "If it's all right with you…"

"Of course, it is." She smiled warmly at Molly. "In fact, if you have something you need to do, Garrett, I'll be glad to keep an eye on her and walk her home anytime you'd like."

He seemed to consider and she dared to hope that she wouldn't be subjected to…overwhelmed by…his continuing presence.

"I think I'll stay awhile, too," he decided.

It was all she could do not to groan. "But—"

"I think I should try to get to know your cats a little better," he interrupted smoothly. "If we're going to coexist peacefully this summer, I should at least make the effort, don't you think?"

"Well, yes, I suppose, but—"

"And you should make a similar effort toward the dogs," he went on firmly.

Her stomach clenched into a knot of protest. "Not a chance."

"Never say never." Climbing out of the car, he came around to open first Molly's door, then Brooke's. When both had climbed out, he added, "I'll bet you could get over your unreasoning hatred of dogs if you'd try."

"It isn't unreasoning and it—it isn't even hatred. It's fear." She bit her lip, sorry she'd said so much.

He took the key from her fingers and unlocked the front door, holding it open for her and Molly to enter. "Tell me about it," he suggested gently.

"There's nothing worth telling." Turning to Molly, Brooke caught the little girl's hands. "Would you like to play with Gable and Lombard or would you prefer to meet some of my other guests? I'll bet you'd like Mrs. Swann's cat, Pookie, and he loves to be petted."

Garrett gave Brooke a cocky grin, then said to Molly, "What guy doesn't."

Molly just smiled and nodded. Ah, to be young and innocent!

While Molly played with the cats, Brooke found herself once again playing hostess to the little girl's father. Somehow she found him more...*dangerous* in this familiar setting than in the sunny ambience of downtown Boulder. Over tall glasses of ice tea, she regarded him warily.

He'd grown quiet over the past half hour, as if his entire mood had changed. She wondered why; she hoped she wouldn't find out why, because she didn't think she'd like the answer.

"Brooke," he began, sounding unusually serious, "there's something—"

"Not now, Garrett," she said too brightly. "Why don't you tell me what you think of Boulder? You haven't seen nearly all there is to see, but I think you can get the idea—"

"Forget Boulder." He leaned forward and placed

his glass on the table between them in her sitting room. "I really need to talk to you about something a lot more important."

She leaned away from him. "I don't think I want to hear this," she said in a strangled voice.

"I wish I didn't have to insist, but I do. I've already put it off too long." Without the ready smile, his face looked leaner, harder. "What's your price, Brooke?"

"My price for *what*?"

It just popped out before she had a chance to think. But her inane comment had an unexpected side benefit: he smiled.

"Ah," he said gently, "are we opening this up for suggestions?"

"No, of course not." Embarrassed, she chewed on her lower lip. "You're talking about…my home?"

He nodded. "This house and the land that goes with it. I want it, Brooke—I need it and I intend to have it. I don't know why Cora left it to you but it's yours and we'll start there."

"I don't know why she did, either."

He looked into her eyes as if trying to make up his mind about the veracity of her statement. Finally he said, "We'll let that go for the moment."

"Gosh, thanks for nothing."

"Don't get sarcastic." But he grinned at her, adding, "I'd just as soon be pleasant about this if we can manage it."

"I couldn't agree more," she said with relief.

"Then name your price," he said again.

"My home is not for sale, Garrett."

"Everything's for sale, Brooke."

She shook her head stubbornly. "Don't do this," she whispered. "Don't break Miss Cora's heart."

"I couldn't possibly. Miss Cora is dead." His face was implacable.

"But she was your great-aunt, your own flesh and blood. She didn't want you to sell what she left you to the highest bidder."

"What difference does it make now what she wanted? She's gone. She'll never know."

"Maybe—maybe not. But according to her will—"

"I'm an attorney. Do you think I'll have the slightest trouble breaking that will?"

That jolted her. "Why go to the trouble?" she argued. "Do you...do you need the money that bad?"

She'd blurted that last part out, only afterward realizing he might be offended. He wasn't, she saw at once; his expression didn't alter.

He spoke almost gently. "It's not the money. I don't need the money, not the way you mean. But I also don't need the aggravation that hanging on to this place would inevitably mean to me."

"Then turn it into a cat shelter, which was her second choice," Brooke urged.

"I'm much too practical to do any such thing." He shifted restlessly in his seat in the overstuffed chair, the first indication he'd given that he might not be as cool about this subject as his words indicated. "Look, Brooke, I only came here this summer because...well, because I felt I needed some time alone with Molly."

"That's commendable, but—"

"No buts. I didn't have to come here at all, regardless of any old will."

Her head drooped. "Then you'd made up your mind before you ever got here?"

"Of course." He didn't smile.

"And you weren't even the tiniest little bit curious about your great-aunt?"

He shrugged. "Only in a negative way. I think I told you that she was never mentioned in the family."

"Yes, but that wasn't her fault. She—"

"Brooke, stop romanticizing everything!" For the first time, he looked truly annoyed. "You see everything in black and white but the world is full of shades of gray. Cora wasn't some persecuted angel."

"I never suggested she was. But my goodness, what was the awful crime she committed? She ran away from home at the age of fifteen—fifteen! Surely she could be forgiven for that."

His dark brows rose. "You're right, and you're also wrong. In the first place, she wasn't fifteen, she was seventeen."

"What? But she said she made her first movie at sixteen!"

"Actually, she was almost eighteen."

"But why would she lie?" To me, at least. Why would she lie to me? Brooke wondered.

He shrugged. "By the time she told you that, she'd probably forgotten what the truth was," he suggested.

Struggling with this new bit of information, which she didn't for a moment doubt was true, she struggled to pick up the argument. "Okay, she was two years older than I thought. But that's still too young to be permanently tossed out of the family just for running away."

"Even if she didn't leave Chicago alone?"

A cold chill gripped Brooke's heart. Slowly she looked up from perusal of her hands gripped in her lap. Her gaze met his and she thought she saw regret.

"Who did she leave with?"

"Her older sister's fiancé."

"She had a sister? But I thought—" She broke off to stare at him, appalled.

He nodded. "Her sister's name was Maude, and that's what precipitated the family quarrel, or so my father told me. Cora's father finally tracked her down but whatever was said, he never repeated. When he returned home without her, he and Maude were locked in the library for a long time. When they came out, they informed the entire family that Cora's name was never to be mentioned again. While he lived, I gather that it never was."

"How awful." Brooke didn't know why she believed him so implicitly but she did. Somehow she didn't think he'd lie to her. Tease her, intrigue her, confuse her, but not lie to her. "W-what about Maude?" she asked at last. "Is she still alive?"

He shook his head. "But Cora obviously didn't know that, since she left her estate to her sister. As Maude's heir, I was next in line."

"Did she ever marry?"

"No."

"Did she forgive her sister?"

"No."

"And neither did you," Brooke said with a sigh.

"My feelings aren't really important, except that I'm as loyal to Maude as you are to Cora." He shrugged. "I know that's not what you wanted to hear, but I think you prefer the truth."

"Yes." But did she? Although her faith in Miss Cora's veracity had been severely shaken, her love was as strong as ever. A sudden thought occurred to her. "Was Robert Browne the man who broke Maude's heart?"

"That's right."

"Garrett, doesn't it count for anything that he and Miss Cora were married for fifty years, until the day he died? I don't think she ever looked at another man. It really was true love."

He looked startled. "I knew he married her but..." He frowned. He shook his head, his bottom lip thrusting out stubbornly. "That doesn't change anything. Which brings me back to my original offer. Name your price, Brooke. I'll have a hell of a time selling my majority if you don't cooperate, but believe me, I'll find a way if I have to."

"My answer's still no." She lifted her chin and met his steady gaze. "Miss Cora wanted me to have a place of my own, where I could care for her cats when she was no longer around to do it—she said so in her will."

His beautiful amber eyes narrowed. "If you think I'm going to be thwarted by a pair of *cats*—"

She resisted the impulse to flinch before his wrath. "No, you're going to be thwarted by *me*. I'll never give in—I'll fight you every step of the way, Garrett Jackson!"

"You may at that, but you won't win." He spoke

with absolute finality. "I'm going to close this chapter for Miss Maude's sake."

"And I'm going to keep this chapter open for Miss Cora's sake."

They glowered at each other, neither willing to look away first. As the intensity grew, so did the electric attraction arcing between them. Almost imperceptibly, Brooke felt herself leaning toward him, sensed him leaning toward her—

"No!" Abruptly she stood up, breaking the force field that had held them captive. "I'm not going to let you intimidate me."

"That's what you call it?"

His voice had taken on a lazy, sexy quality that made her shiver. She started toward the front door. "Never mind what I call it. We have nothing more to say to each other."

"But—"

"Go home, Garrett! Can't you see that I've had just about all I can take?" She was reaching for the door as she spoke, opening it. A furry streak darted between her legs, startling her, making her yelp with surprise. "Who was that?"

Molly, with Pookie lolling across her lap, said helpfully, "I think that was Deadeye Dick."

"Oh, dear!" Brooke looked outside but failed to spot the black cat. "Dick gets a little crazy once in a while but I'll find him." She added a muttered, "I hope!" Deadeye Dick, so named because he'd lost an eye during his days as an alley cat, was completely unpredictable. When the mood was on him, there was no telling what he might do.

Garrett gestured to Molly. "Come along, sweetheart. We've got to go home now."

"But—"

"I'm sorry, but it's time."

Molly rose reluctantly. Without waiting for them to get organized, Brooke stepped outside and looked around. Deadeye was nowhere to be seen. She started up the path toward the mansion, calling out to him.

She'd nearly reached the tall Glennhaven gate by the time she spotted him. The silly cat was sitting smack-dab in the middle of the trail, looking up at something completely fascinating in a tall pine tree.

"There you are!" she scolded, marching toward him. "You naughty cat! You shouldn't be wandering around out here all by—"

The gate slammed open, interrupting her monologue, and Larry the terrier burst through. Within two strides he was in full voice, yapping his silly head off and aiming his bulky body straight at the cat.

Who sat there as if paralyzed, only his fur rising to the danger of the occasion. Screaming, Brooke ran toward her cat, arms outstretched. She was aware of Garrett behind her, aware of the pounding of his feet, but she dared not wait for his help.

She and Larry reached the cat at almost the same moment. All she could see was Deadeye, frozen in his tracks, and the powerful jaws of that horrible dog reaching for him. Without giving personal danger a thought, she made a grab for her cat—but came up with the dog. Larry let out a quivering yelp that sounded as if he were being murdered, and put on the brakes.

Mrs. Sisk rushed through the gate. "What in the name of heaven—"

"My cat!" Brooke shouted, releasing Larry and looking around frantically. "Where's my cat?"

Garrett pointed. "I think he shinnied up that tree. Are you all right, Brooke? It's not too smart to come between two animals like that. You could have been—"

Mrs. Sisk interrupted. "Mr. Jackson, what is the meaning of this? Are we facing an entire summer spent trying to keep cats and dogs apart? Because if we are, I'm prepared to pack my things and go straight back to Chicago!"

"Now, Mrs. Sisk, we'll figure out a way to avoid this kind of thing," Garrett promised. "If we'll all just be a little bit patient—"

"Patient!" Brooke almost shouted the word. "How can I be patient? Those dogs have got to go, Garrett. That's the only solution."

"Not the *only* solution." He regarded her with narrow eyes. "The cats could go."

"Or *I* could go." Mrs. Sisk thrust herself squarely in the middle of the quarrel again with her thinly veiled threat. "I can take Molly with me, back to Chicago where she belongs. This is no place for an impressionable child, as I told you quite clearly before we ever came here. Why don't you admit you've made a terrible mistake?"

"Because—" Garrett's eyes went wide with sudden concern. "Where *is* the impressionable child?"

"Oh, dear," Brooke wailed. "Have we upset Molly?" What an awful situation: a frantic cat, an angry dog and an upset child. She whirled, her anxious gaze seeking the little girl.

And finding her almost at once, seated on the exposed root of a tree. Deadeye Dick reclined in her arms and Larry lay beside her, his chin on her lap. Cat and dog glared into each other's eyes but neither made a move to renew hostilities—at least for the moment.

CHAPTER SIX

IT TOOK a few minutes to sort everything out. When they had, Mrs. Sisk, her mouth a grim line of disapproval, hustled Molly back inside the gated yard. When the two were out of sight, Brooke turned to Garrett, who was kneeling to restrain Larry.

"Mrs. Sisk is going to quit," Brooke predicted.

"No, she's not." He looked equally certain of his opinion. "It's all for show. If there's one thing I'm sure of, it's that she'd never leave Molly."

"She doesn't think she'll have to."

That got his attention. "What's that supposed to mean?" he demanded.

Brooke spoke thoughtfully. "Didn't you hear her? She intends to take Molly back to Chicago with her."

"Not a chance," he said flatly. "I'd never permit such a thing." His lips thinned out in a line of displeasure. "You've misread the woman, Brooke. She won't quit. But even if she did, she'd never expect me to let her take Molly back home."

How did she get into these things? Brooke wondered. *This was none of her business.* She'd vowed to keep her distance from the Jacksons, for heaven's sake. "Have it your way," she said. Shifting Deadeye Dick from one arm to the other, she turned away, unable to resist adding in an undertone he couldn't possibly hear, "But you're wrong."

He heard. "Wanna bet?"

She stopped short; the man must have incredible hearing. Slowly she turned to face him where he still knelt beside the now-docile dog. His strong, handsome face was tilted up to her and the light of challenge gleamed in his beautiful golden eyes.

"Yes," she surprised herself by saying. "Yes, Mr. Wise Guy, I want to bet!"

"You do? Gotcha!" With a final glance at the cat safe in her arms, he released the terrier and rose to his feet in one smooth motion. A speculative smile touched his mouth, attractively tilting his lips at the corners.

"Now hang on a minute!" She took a hasty step back. "That was just a figure of speech."

He shook his head, taunting her. "You can't back out now. You just bet me that Mrs. Sisk wouldn't last the summer and I took you up on it. So what're the stakes?"

"The what?"

"What's at stake here?" he explained patiently. "What does the winner win—and what does the loser lose?"

"I have no idea."

He rubbed his hands together as if in anticipation and she found herself staring at the long, strong fingers. His hands, like the rest of him, were graceful and well-formed.

"Then I'll help you out," he offered. "How about breakfast in—"

"You've got the most one-track mind of any man I ever met," she wailed.

"And you're easier to tease than any woman *I* ever met," he countered. "Com' on, Brooke, lighten up. We're both adults here. A little extracurricular activity wouldn't do either of us any harm."

Oh, no? She cast about frantically for a way to distract him, something she could offer in case she lost— which she wouldn't. Maybe she should call his bluff; it might be worth it to—

And then she flashed on an image so unsettling that she gasped: herself, propped up by a multitude of pillows in her own bed while Garrett Jackson approached bearing a tray of breakfast delicacies and wearing a smile—

This was a lose-lose situation for her. Garrett and a bed, hers as much as his, would be an explosive combination.

He grinned as if he could read her thoughts. "I'm waiting," he said, crossing his arms across his broad chest.

"Okay," she said hastily. "How about—how about this? If I lose, I'll...I'll take you and Molly on a Fourth of July picnic. How about that?"

His eyes narrowed with speculation. "Picnic, huh? And if I lose I'll serve you breakfast in—"

"Garrett!" She longed to stamp her foot in frustration. "You will never see the inside of my bedroom so give it up!"

"Wanna bet?"

"I want you to—"

"Name it."

"Leave me alone!"

"That's not what you want."

Stepping close to her, he caught her by the upper arms. She looked at him helplessly, clutching the cat to her chest. An increasingly familiar weakness flooded through her, making her knees weak, shredding her resistance.

The teasing light had left his eyes and he looked at her intently. "Drop the damn cat so I can kiss you," he ordered in a husky voice.

Her knees might have buckled completely if he hadn't been holding her upright. She swallowed hard and said a squeaky, "No!" Unfortunately, she also squeezed Deadeye Dick so tightly that he let out a startled protest and leapt from her arms, taking her defenses with him.

Garrett leaned toward her. "Nice cat," he murmured just before his lips touched hers.

The man's kiss was pure magic. Brooke melted against him with a sigh, sliding her arms around his lean waist and tilting her face toward his. Eyes closed, she surrendered without so much as a fight.

When at last the long, leisurely kiss ended, she heard him draw a deep, ragged breath. Then she felt his mouth against her closed eyelids. She almost groaned with pleasure—until he spoke.

"Give up, Brooke," he murmured against her temple. "I've got my heart set on having breakfast in bed with you and when I want something that much—"

"You rat!" With superhuman effort, she shoved out of his arms. "If you win our bet, I'll take you and your daughter on a picnic. If I win, you'll...you'll leave me alone!"

"Whoa!" He didn't look the least bit impressed by

her outburst. "How can I leave you alone when you're living right under my nose? If you'd be reasonable and sell your land to me—"

His meaning slashed at her like a whip. He was coming on to her in hopes that when she'd had enough, she'd sell out just to get away from him. He was, quite simply, trying to scare her into compliance with his wishes by turning her own weakness against her.

"How dare you!" Before she could stop herself, she drew back to do something she'd never done in her life: strike another human being. Before she could slap his deceitful face, his own hand darted out to catch her wrist in midmotion.

He was no longer teasing, nor smiling. "Brooke, what is it? What set you off?"

"You know perfectly well!" She yanked her wrist from his grip and massaged skin tingling from contact with his. "All right, Garrett, you've made a fool of me. But you're not going to scare me away so you may as well stop trying."

"You think that's what's going on here, that I'm trying to scare you away?"

"It's obvious!"

He shook his head slowly. "Brooke, are you really that naive or are you just playing games? I'm not trying to scare you away, I'm trying to...entice you."

"Entice me?" She frowned, trying to figure out his meaning. "You mean, to sell my home?"

His laugh sounded incredulous. "First things first. I'm trying to entice you into my bed, sweetheart." He slipped one hand around the curve of her neck, beneath her hair. "How much more honest can I be?"

She twisted away from his touch. "In that case, I honestly don't think I can work with you anymore."

His brows rose in question. "Meaning?"

"That I won't be helping you sort Miss Cora's things. Under the circumstances, I couldn't possibly." *There*! That would get her out of this mess. If she didn't see him, she could put him completely out of her mind.

"Hypocrite."

"What? Why would you say that?"

He thrust his hands deep into his pockets, as if to keep from grabbing her again. "I thought you were such a big fan of Miss Cora's."

"I am. What has that got to do with anything?"

"It has everything to do with it. Didn't you jump all over me for not adhering to the letter of her will?"

"I—why, I—"

"And didn't her will specifically request that you give me every assistance?"

"Yes, but she couldn't possibly have known what a—what a jerk you'd turn out to be." ·

He laughed. "That has yet to be determined," he said airily. "I just don't see how you can criticize me for ignoring Miss Cora's wishes and then turn around and do the same thing yourself. But if that's the way you want to be, there's nothing I can do about it. I'll just have to handle it all myself." He half turned toward the house. "Maybe I should just call in one of those companies that handles estate sales and get rid of the whole—"

"No!" She clasped her hands in distress. "Please don't do that. I'll help."

His quick smile said he'd never doubted it. "That's great."

"But only on the condition—"

"Do I hear Molly calling?" He cupped his ear toward the gate, his motions exaggerated. "I'd love to stay and chat but—"

"Garrett! I mean it. You've got to stop—"

"We'll get going tomorrow morning, okay?" He edged down the path, pretending great concern for what lay behind the iron gate. "We'll have lunch, then get to work."

"Okay, but—"

He was gone and she was talking to a pine forest.

Brooke sat in a comfortable overstuffed chair in one of the Catty-Corner's "cat suites," a roly-poly gray kitten tumbling around her feet in pursuit of a leather mouse. The kitten, Misty, batted the mouse across the room where it landed at the feet of Snookims, a mature calico with haughty demeanor.

Snookims gave the kitten a disdainful glance and leapt lightly up to the viewing shelf before the window, pointedly turning her back on the goings-on.

Brooke reached down to ruffle the kitten's fur, then pick him up to nestle on her lap. Upon her return from her clash with Garrett Jackson, she'd thrown herself into a routine she loved and that never failed her: caring for the cats.

But now, hours later, everything was shipshape, all felines fed and watered, comfortable and happy in sparkling-clean quarters. All that remained was the best part: offering each an individual helping of love and attention.

Uncharacteristically, she found herself doing that automatically, unable to pull her thoughts away from the Jacksons, father and daughter, and the disagreeable nanny.

But mostly she thought about Garrett, a dangerous man with a one-track mind and an uncanny ability to sense her weaknesses and exploit them. He'd unerringly used her feelings for his great-aunt against her and now she was committed to spending even more time in his presence.

So be it, she decided, tickling Misty's furry tummy and enjoying the kitten's purring approval. She would insist—no, demand!—that everything between them be kept on a strictly impersonal basis. She would not be another notch on his bedpost like the unfortunate Caroline and Dee-Dee.

No more talk about "breakfast in bed"; the only breakfasts in bed around here would go to the cats!

For a week Brooke clung to her resolve. Each day she walked, reluctant but determined, to the mansion. Cloaked in a mantle of reserve, she went about her duties, helping to sort and catalog the acquisitions of a lifetime.

The movie memorabilia alone was staggering, both in quality and quantity. Autographed photographs of long-ago stars, movie posters in mint condition, artifacts from films such as Valentino's boots from *The Four Horsemen of the Apocalypse*, even the forty-inch strand of perfect pearls worn by Miss Cora herself in her final film in 1927.

When Brooke unearthed the pearls casually stored in a velvet pouch in the bottom of a cardboard box, she read the attached tag and gasped. She'd seen the film in which they'd featured prominently a dozen times and felt as if she held a piece of true history in her hands.

"What is it?" Across the room stacking leather-bound books by subject, Garrett looked up.

Wordlessly she held up the strand of pearls for his perusal. They cascaded across her palm like a fabulous waterfall.

He didn't look impressed. "You want them?"

"I wasn't hinting."

He shrugged as if that point were immaterial. "Keep them." He turned back to the task at hand.

Brooke bit her lip, her gaze going from the man to the pearls and back again. She should. He was so indifferent to this entire process. She'd been biting her tongue to keep from being openly critical, which she couldn't afford to be.

At least he'd not pressed her on a personal level. At first pleased, she'd grown resentful that he'd given up so easily. Was she all that easy to dismiss?

Who was she kidding? She couldn't keep anything so valuable as these pearls. She sighed. "Thanks," she forced herself to say, "but I really couldn't."

He paused, holding several books. "Why not?"

"They're real, Garrett. They must be worth...I don't know, thousands of dollars."

"So?"

"So—" She floundered. "It wouldn't be right."

"If you don't take them, I'll only sell them," he said, not looking as if he cared much one way or the other. "It's up to you."

He went back to work but she couldn't, not yet. They'd had this conversation several times already. He'd offered her furniture, jewelry, personal items such as letters, all without obvious strings attached.

The operative word, she knew, was "obvious." He was offering her...was the proper word "bribes"? He wanted to buy her inheritance and would use any method at his disposal to that end.

But he never said so. He never tied any of the proffered gifts to her acquiescence to his demands. Which, of course, only made it worse. Her sense of honor and fairness would not allow her to take the gifts he offered without giving something in return.

What he wanted, she couldn't give—neither her home nor her virtue. With a sigh, she coiled the pearls back inside the velvet pouch and set it aside.

She couldn't be bought. She might have to fight his undeniable attraction, but she couldn't be bought.

"Mrs. O'Hara says, 'Come to lunch.'"

Brooke looked up from her examination of crumbling press clippings in an old leather scrapbook to find Molly standing in the doorway, her dog beside her. She looked somehow pale and wan, Brooke thought, as if she weren't really enjoying her summer vacation very much.

Molly added a plaintive, "Please?"

Garrett, seated behind a massive mahogany desk,

stood. "Yes, Brooke," he agreed. "Come have lunch with us."

She'd faced the same dilemma every day she'd been here: invitations she felt she must refuse. If she were to keep her association with Garrett on any kind of an even keel, she must avoid purely social situations. So she smiled and said, "Thank you, but I'd better go home for lunch so I can check on the cats."

Quick tears sprang to Molly's eyes, tears Brooke had never seen there before. Their appearance sent a quick shaft of sympathy through her.

"P-*please* come," the little girl stammered. "I *like* you, Ms. Brooke."

"I like you, too, Molly, but—"

"If you come, I'll eat my broccoli," Molly bargained, darting a quick glance at Garrett.

Brooke gathered broccoli must be a topic of considerable discussion in the Jackson household. "You should eat your broccoli whether I come to lunch or not," she said, trying not to sound as if she were lecturing. "It's not only good for you but it tastes wonderful."

Molly made a face. "Chocolate tastes wonderful. Broccoli tastes...green."

Garrett came around the desk, grinning. "How would *you* know? You've never tasted it."

"That's 'cause I already know I hate it." Molly's lower lip thrust out. "Mrs. Sisk makes me eat all kinds of stuff but I won't eat that!" She turned big, beseeching eyes on Brooke. "Except if you'll come," she added, a tremble in her voice. "Mrs. Sisk says I shouldn't keep bothering you but…but…Mrs. O'Hara said I could ask and…and…'' She stumbled to a halt.

So Mrs. Sisk doesn't want me to stay for lunch, Brooke translated. She spared a quick glance at Garrett and found him watching her closely but without comment.

She squared her shoulders. ''Okay, Molly, I'll be glad to stay for lunch,'' she said. ''Thank you for asking—and don't forget your promise to eat your broccoli!''

The brilliance of Molly's smile nearly eclipsed Brooke's many misgivings.

Garrett was astonished at his ability to read Brooke like a book without even trying. He'd known instinctively that if he joined his daughter in urging their prickly neighbor to stay for lunch, she'd feel duty-bound to refuse. But if he stayed out of it and let Molly carry the fight, she'd have to give in…and she had.

Following her down the stairs, he found himself intrigued by the curve of her cheek, visible when she turned her head slightly to speak to Molly, by the slender strength of her shoulders and her graceful carriage. Even in faded jeans and equally faded red T-shirt, she looked wonderful.

Must be the novelty, he mused. It had been a long time…maybe never…since an attractive woman had declined to make an effort to attract his attention.

They'd been working side by side for several days now, and true to his pledge—made to himself, not to her—he'd kept his distance.

But even at that distance, he found himself watching her, always measuring and assessing. He would identify her Achilles' heel; everyone had one. When he did, he'd have her land, her house...*her*, he didn't doubt. She was as attracted to him as he was to her and when the time was right.

It's all a little game, he thought, following her through the door to the smaller of the two dining rooms, a sunny breakfast chamber off the kitchen itself. She'd have no cause to regret his success, for he was prepared to overpay her shamelessly for what he wanted.

But he could wait. He had the entire summer. He'd play her little games...at least for a while.

Smiling, he held her chair before moving to take his place at the head of the table.

Brooke was greeted effusively by Mrs. O'Hara and coolly by Mrs. Sisk. Trying to keep everything low-key and pleasant, Brooke tried to remain in the background, but Molly made that nearly impossible.

The girl seemed to have turned into a regular chatterbox. She talked about her dog, the swing Garrett had hung from a tree on the edge of the formal garden, the fun she'd had in the swimming pool.

"Will you come swim with me?" she asked Brooke, poking at her salad without enthusiasm. "I swim pretty good."

"I'll bet you do." Brooke stifled a groan. She'd never realized how frequently the word "bet" crept into her vocabulary until Garrett made such a point of it. She cast him a surreptitious glance, which he didn't seem to notice.

Mrs. Sisk cleared her throat. "Eat your salad, Molly," she commanded.

"Yes, ma'am." Molly speared a tiny shred of carrot and popped it into her mouth. To Brooke she added, "Can you swim?"

"Yes."

"That's good. Gart swims real good, too. He—"

"Molly! Children should be seen and not heard at the table."

"Yes, Mrs. Sisk."

Brooke clenched her teeth hard. Knowing she shouldn't, she still couldn't help wishing Molly would rebel against the woman's iron hand.

As if sensing hostility, Mrs. Sisk went on in a pompous tone, "Molly's eating habits leave a great deal to be desired. The older she gets, the less balanced her diet. She'll hardly touch vegetables, although when she was younger she—"

"When she was younger," Garrett cut in, an edge to his voice, "she had no choice. Now she does."

"Are you suggesting that she be allowed to eat only what she chooses?" Mrs. Sisk demanded.

"I'm suggesting," he replied in the same unruffled tone, "that nobody likes to have every bite monitored. If we just leave Molly alone, I'm sure she'll come around."

Mrs. O'Hara, who had entered quietly, picked up his salad plate with a quick, questioning glance. Sitting across the table, Brooke tried to think of a way to lighten the mood—and failed.

A superior smile touched the nanny's face. "Your experience with children is somewhat limited," she said condescendingly. "You can safely—"

"Here's lunch!" Mrs. O'Hara bustled back in, carrying a tray which she placed on a sideboard. "Roast chicken, rice pilaf and broccoli—what could be nicer?"

Mrs. Sisk grimaced. "Molly detests broccoli," she announced. "I've successfully gotten her to eat almost anything else, but never broccoli."

Mrs. O'Hara placed plates before Molly and Brooke. "Perhaps this time will be different," she suggested.

Mrs. Sisk rolled her eyes in response. Brooke could see her squaring her shoulders as if preparing to do battle—and with a child, for heaven's sake. It was too unfair.

Somebody ought to do something about it.

Molly watched and listened without comment. When all were served and Mrs. O'Hara had left the room, everybody turned to the girl as one.

"Molly..." Mrs. Sisk began in a warning tone.

"Mrs. Sisk," Garrett said more sharply.

"Ms. Brooke?"

Molly's eyes were pleading. What Brooke read in them was, *Now what*?

Without thinking, Brooke patted the little girl's hand. "Life's too short to spend it arguing about *broccoli*," she announced with a smile. "Give it a try, okay, Molly?" She cast a quick glance at Mrs. Sisk and added, "For me?"

Molly looked relieved. "For you, Ms. Brooke."

She looked down at the offending vegetable, took a deep breath and picked it up by the stalk. She took a big bite off the ruffly end and chewed. A look of surprise crossed her small face.

"Pretty good, huh?" Brooke smiled and took a hasty bite of her own broccoli, not wanting Molly to feel as if she were all alone in this. "It's my very favorite vegetable so I'm glad you like it, too."

"I don't *love* it." Molly swallowed hard. "Do I have to eat it all?"

Brooke patted the girl's shoulder. "You don't have to eat a bit more than you want."

Mrs. Sisk leaned forward. "It's not your prerogative to tell this child what she will or won't eat."

"But I wasn't—" Brooke fought to control her anger. This woman just brought out all her protective instincts.

Molly glanced anxiously from one to the other. "I'll eat it all! Don't make her go home, Mrs. Sisk." Molly crammed broccoli into her mouth with both hands. Tears welled in her eyes.

"That's enough!" Garrett rose to his feet, magnificent in his anger. "Molly, stop that! Brooke is absolutely right. You don't have to eat a bite more than you want, now or ever."

"Mr. Jackson!" Mrs. Sisk also stood up, her expression unrelenting. "I cannot allow you to undermine my authority."

"In that case, you're discharged."

An audible gasp greeted this pronouncement. Brooke reached for Molly's hand and they both waited with bated breath to see what would happen next.

Mrs. Sisk was apparently rendered speechless for she simply gaped at Garrett. He sat back down, returned his napkin to his lap and picked up his fork.

The nanny leaned forward, bracing the heels of her hands on the table. "Am I to understand that I have just been *fired*?"

Garrett, in complete control, looked up from his roast chicken. "Certainly not," he said. "I simply think it's time you returned to Chicago, which you obviously prefer to Colorado."

"Oh." Mrs. Sisk looked confused for a moment. "Then you are sending Molly and me—"

"Not Molly. You. Molly will stay here with me for the summer. Think of this as...as a vacation. When I return to Chicago in the fall, we'll talk."

The woman's eyes widened. "I can't believe what I'm hearing. You can't possibly get along without me."

"I can only try," Garrett said gently. "We'll discuss this later, Mrs. Sisk." He cast a significant glance at Molly, who listened wide-eyed. She obviously didn't understand what was going on—that freedom was, in fact, at hand. "Please—" He gestured. "Won't you sit down and enjoy your lunch?"

To Brooke's surprise, Mrs. Sisk slowly lowered herself into her chair and picked up her napkin. She looked...well, she looked as if she were in a state of shock. She glanced up, catching Brooke watching her.

"How did you do that?" Mrs. Sisk asked in a flat voice.

"D-do what?" Brooke stammered, feeling as if she'd just been a party to something she shouldn't have seen.

"Get Molly to eat her broccoli."

"Oh, that." Brooke chewed at her lower lip. "To be honest, it was her idea."

"*Her* idea?" The nanny's brows soared.

"She wanted me to stay to lunch and offered to eat her broccoli if I would." Brooke gave Molly a quick little smile of encouragement. "How could I turn down an offer like that?"

"How, indeed." Mrs. Sisk looked stunned. "How, indeed."

Brooke heard the subtext very clearly. *For you, she eats broccoli. For me…*

Mrs. Sisk stood up. "Perhaps you're right, Mr. Jackson. I *do* need a vacation. If you'll excuse me, I'll go pack now."

Not another word was said until she'd left the room.

CHAPTER SEVEN

"OH, MY goodness!" Brooke cast an anxious glance after the retreating nanny, then turned to Garrett. He was calmly eating his lunch, acting for all the world as if nothing had happened. "Garrett!" she exclaimed.

"Later," he said with a significant glance at Molly. She, too, had picked up her fork. Fortunately, she seemed completely undisturbed by what had just happened.

So Brooke followed suit. Ordinarily she'd have enjoyed Mrs. O'Hara's light but excellent lunch, but after what had just happened she could barely taste the food. She was the only one so affected, however, for when Mrs. O'Hara reentered, both Garrett and Molly had cleaned their plates.

The woman glanced around the table with knowing eyes. "Well, Molly, my girl, how would you like to help me prepare the dessert?" she asked heartily. "I'm afraid I just got too busy and now I sure could use some help in the kitchen."

Molly's face brightened. She glanced toward Mrs. Sisk's empty chair as if to ask permission, then at Garrett with a frown. "Can I, Gart?"

He grinned; it softened his entire face. "Sure you can." He added significantly to Mrs. O'Hara, "Take your time.''

Her nod said she understood.

"You win," Garrett announced.

"I win what?" Brooke, who'd been sitting there feeling guilty about her part in all this, glanced at him in surprise.

"You win the bet."

"What in the world are you talking about?" She stared at him, perplexed.

"You said Mrs. Sisk wouldn't last the summer and you were right."

Understanding dawned. "No, Garrett. I said Mrs. Sisk would quit. She didn't quit, you fired her."

He shrugged. "Same difference. She's gone. You still win."

"Now wait a minute!" Why was he so eager to concede defeat? "Technically—"

"You even warned me she'd want to take Molly back with her. That really floored me." He did, indeed, look baffled. "Do I seem that indifferent a father?"

Although spoken lightly, she sensed the seriousness behind his question. "Not at all, Garrett," she said quickly. "I think you're a very good father, or at least, you're trying to be."

His gaze sharpened. "Talk about damning with faint praise."

She'd come too far to stop now. "Let's just say you're as good a father as Molly will let you be," she said gently. "This has been as hard on her as it has on you. She's obviously not ready to accept you as her father yet—she still calls you Gart, for goodness' sake—but that time will come.''

"Do you really think so?"

She heard doubt and hope in the question and her heart went out to him in a way it never had before. "Of course I really think so," she said staunchly. "She needs time with *you,* not with a crabby nanny."

"You're probably right…within reason."

Her antenna prickled. "Which means what?"

"I'm not sure I'm ready to take this on all alone. I don't have much experience in this daddy stuff."

A feeling of unease crept over her. "You won't be all alone. Mrs. O'Hara will be here."

He nodded solemnly but she didn't trust that sparkle in his amber eyes. "Unfortunately, she's already got enough to keep her busy, between the cooking and the cleaning. She won't have time to give Molly the personal attention she deserves—that she needs."

"Oh, I don't think—"

"But you do," he said. "That's one of the things I like best about you. You not only *think,* you think of others first—like Molly, I mean."

"What?" Brooke recoiled against her chair. "I don't know anything about children."

"She likes you," he said with bland assurance.

"And I like her, but—"

"You didn't like Mrs. Sisk."

"Well, no, but—"

"You thought Molly would be better off without her and now she is. Don't you think it's the least you can do to pitch in and—"

"Garrett, stop!" Brooke held up her hands, she hoped not in surrender.

"I'm not asking for so very much," he argued. "It would mean a lot if you could just spend a little time with us each day—with her, I mean."

"I'm busy. I have the cats—"

"Molly loves the cats. She could help you."

"And when I come here—" she gestured around the elegant breakfast room "—it's to work."

He gave her a smile that curled her toes. "You know what they say about all work and no play. Besides, I'll pay you."

"That isn't what's worrying me," she said tartly.

His dark brows rose. "Then what is?"

"Nothing," she said hastily. "I mean—" She sighed. "I don't know what I mean." She met his probing gaze, although it took all her willpower to do so. When she couldn't stand it any longer she blurted, "Do you still intend to ignore the conditions of Miss Cora's will?"

He didn't flinch. "Yes."

She groaned. "Won't you reconsider? She really wanted—"

"What, Brooke? How can you be sure what she really meant in that will? She couldn't possibly have believed she could force me to live in this mausoleum indefinitely. If she wanted it to be a cat sanctuary, why didn't she skip me entirely and make that stipulation?"

Brooke had wondered that herself. She shook her head in frustration. "I don't know, I honestly don't. She was eccentric, Garrett, I'll admit that. But the least we can do is try to carry out her last wishes no matter how peculiar they may seem to us. If you'd just try to see it from her point of view…''

''Is that your price, Brooke?''

She gasped. ''My price for w-what?''

''To help my daughter, of course. If I agree to at least *consider* sticking to the letter of the will, can I count on your support?''

What would she be letting herself in for if she agreed? She adored Molly Jackson but Molly's father was…something else entirely. ''I…''

Molly came skipping through the doorway, a plate of cookies in her hands. ''I put the cookies on the plate and I dipped the apple sauce,'' she exclaimed, apparently referring to the contents of the small bowls carried on a tray by Mrs. O'Hara, coming through the doorway behind her.

Garrett smiled at her delight. ''That's wonderful, Molly. Now that you're such a big girl, there are lots of things you can do.''

Her eyes grew large. ''I can?''

''Sure. For example, you can help Brooke with the cats. Would you like that?''

Molly gave a little hop of delight, bouncing the cookies on the plate but not losing any. ''Oh, yes! I love Ms. Brooke's cats!''

''Dirty trick, Garrett!'' Brooke said it with a smile she hoped would deceive the little girl. ''Using Molly to get your way—''

''Isn't that what you were doing?'' he countered blandly. ''Hey, Molly, do I get one of those cookies?''

Garrett would always get his share of the cookies, Brooke thought, watching Molly pass around the plate—no matter whose cookies they were.

Garrett drove Mrs. Sisk to Denver International Airport that afternoon, returning several hours later. Brooke heard light footsteps on the stair and identified them immediately as his—how, she wasn't quite sure. An electrician had been in and out for the past two hours and she'd never mistaken *his* footsteps for Garrett's.

It was unnerving. She was already off stride before he appeared in the doorway to the library, looking crisp and sexy in white trousers and a blue polo shirt. She found herself wishing she'd forgone her usual jeans and T-shirt apparel.

Molly, quietly playing nearby with an ivory chess set, looked up. "Hi, Gart. I'm helping Ms. Brooke."

"I see that." He crossed the room with those graceful, long-legged strides and knelt beside her. "I took Mrs. Sisk to the airport."

The little girl nodded sagely.

"She wasn't happy here in Colorado, you know."

"I know," Molly said. "She wanted to go home."

"I didn't think you'd mind too much but I'm afraid it didn't occur to me until this very minute to ask you about that."

Molly stared at him, her forehead creased. He'd lost her on that one. He obviously realized it for he added quickly, "I hope you're not too sorry she's gone."

"Not *too* sorry." She sighed. "Mrs. Sisk used to

play with me and read me stories," she added wistfully. "She used to love me."

"She still loves you," Garrett said, his voice husky. "She told me so just before she got on the airplane."

Molly's smile was like sunshine. "I'm glad," she said, "'cause I love her, too." Turning her sweet face toward Brooke, she added, "Will you play with me now, Ms. Brooke?"

"Of course I will, darling," Brooke said around the lump in her throat. Maybe she'd been too hard on Mrs. Sisk.

"And can I play with your cats?"

"Yes, indeed—now, if you'd like." Brooke didn't even bother to glance at Garrett for permission to make the offer. He'd involved her in this, after all.

"Oh, yes! Can I, Gart?"

"Sure. Run and tell Mrs. O'Hara where we're going." He waited until she'd skipped out of the room before turning to Brooke. "You're still sorting that same pile of stuff?"

She glanced down at the papers and files spread out around her on the floor. "It's all so interesting," she apologized. "I spend too much time reading. For example—" she lifted a thick folder "—these are copies of some of her movie contracts. They're fascinating."

"You don't have to explain to me." He cocked his head and looked down at her, a quizzical expression on his face. "There's plenty of time."

"Not really." She jumped up, brushing off her jeans self-consciously. Her pale pink T-shirt had ridden up and she smoothed it over her hips. "Molly's waiting to visit the cats."

"Okay, but first let's work out the details for tomorrow."

"Tomorrow?" She had no idea what he was talking about.

"It's the Fourth of July," he proclaimed.

"And?"

"I'm prepared to pay off my gambling debt," he said with a conspiratorial wink.

She was painfully aware of the wave of heat in her cheeks. "What in the world are you talking about?"

"You won the bet—Mrs. Sisk is gone. I owe you an Independence Day picnic, remember?"

"Wait a minute." She dredged up a memory she'd rather forget. "Whether or not I actually won is open to debate, but even if I did..." She pursed her lips in thought. "As I recall, if you won, you got a picnic, and if I won, I got peace and quiet—from you! Obviously that's now impossible so let's call the whole thing off."

"Hey, I wagered a picnic and you won. Mrs. O'Hara has everything in hand."

She raised one brow skeptically. "Already? Mrs. Sisk is barely out the door."

He grinned. "How much time does it take? Mrs. O'Hara is preparing the picnic and all I need from you is a time to pick you up. Have you given any thought to where we're going?"

"It's your picnic," she reminded him.

"But this is your turf—Colorado, and especially Glennhaven. You pick."

She gave in with a sigh. "Okay. There are some lovely picnic sites within easy walking distance, if that's all right with you. We can carry our lunch in backpacks.''

''Sounds great.''

''Why don't we meet outside at the gate about...eleven o'clock?''

''Molly and I will be there with bells on.''

''Okay.'' She edged toward the door. ''I'll see you there, then.''

Her effort to dismiss him failed, for he followed her through the door. She gave him a suspicious glance.

He grinned. ''Didn't I mention? Since you won't be around to tell me what to do this afternoon, I might as well go along with you and Molly.''

She'd have groaned if Molly hadn't appeared at the foot of the stairs, looking up with a happy, eager expression.

The cats, both residents and guests, were as curious about Molly as she was about them. With the screen door firmly locked to ward off defections, Brooke let the little girl make friends with the entire feline population.

''She's practically a Pied Piper,'' she said approvingly to Garrett, who'd been doing his not-too-effective best to remain aloof.

Gable curled his bulky body around Garrett's ankle, purring noisily. ''Hard to believe she's a Jackson.'' He shuddered but made no move to shove the cat away.

''Why? Are all Jacksons cat haters?'' she asked

lightly. Bending down, she lifted Deadeye Dick for a little cuddling.

"Pretty much." Gable strolled away and Garrett seemed to relax a little. "It's kind of a funny story, actually."

"Funny?"

"Funny as in strange, maybe even a little sad. When Great-aunt Cora ran away with Great-aunt Maude's fiancé, she also took the family cat. Maude took that as a personal repudiation, apparently. Cats were strictly off-limits after that. We always had plenty of dogs around when I was growing up, but never a cat."

"It was hardly the cat's fault," Brooke said indignantly. "You might give them another chance."

"Yeah, like you're willing to give dogs another chance?" Reaching down, he scooped up the gray kitten and lifted her to face level. "What's this little character's name?"

"Misty."

Garrett rubbed the kitten's ears. "See? I'm overcoming the aversion of a lifetime—for you."

She had to laugh and some of the stiffness that had gripped her shoulders dissolved. "Maybe there's hope for you yet," she said lightly. "I commend you for finally seeing the light. Cats *are* superior to dogs."

"No way!" He rubbed the kitten's chin with his forefinger and the little creature purred furiously. "A dog is man's best friend."

"Not anymore. More people have cats for pets than dogs."

"I don't believe it!" He looked completely astonished, not to mention dubious.

She nodded. "Cats outnumber dogs as pets. I read it in a newspaper years ago."

"But why?" He frowned and put the kitten back on the floor. "Dogs are loyal and faithful. They'll bring your slippers and bite burglars. Cats just spit in your eye."

That made Brooke laugh. "But you can leave a cat alone for a day or two and he can take care of himself," she argued. "A dog will trash the place."

"But dogs are always glad to see you when you get home. They'll come when you call and forgive anything. They'll wag their tails and lick your hand and eat your leftovers."

She gave a haughty sniff. "How can you respect an animal with such a total lack of discrimination? Cats have too much integrity to grovel."

They laughed together, and before she could resume the light banter he said too seriously, "But none of this explains why you dislike dogs so violently."

"It's not violently."

"No? You actually flinch every time Baron or Larry walks into the room. Why, Brooke?"

She turned away to place the cat on a perch before the window. "I don't really like to talk about it," she admitted.

"Were you bitten?"

Her chin snapped up. "And then some. I'll carry the scars as long as I live."

He simply looked at her with an expression of enormous sympathy. Then he said, "But you can't condemn all dogs for what one did."

"I don't. A few years later—" She shuddered. "I don't want to talk about this, Garrett."

For a moment he seemed on the verge of protest, but after a quick glance at Molly swinging a feather toy to the delight of the younger cats, he nodded. "This isn't the time and place."

"That's not what I meant, although you're right. I don't intend to talk about it *ever*." She turned to him with an artificially bright smile. "Would you like a glass of ice tea? I think I can use one, and maybe Molly would like juice."

"I'd like—"

"Those are your choices, Garrett," she said sharply. "Tea or juice."

He shrugged. "Tea, by all means."

But she could see beneath his easy acquiescence that the subject was not closed permanently.

They were drinking ice tea in the sitting room, Molly nearby with Lombard on her lap, when a knock of the door intruded. A voice followed. "Brooke, it's John! I've got something for you."

It was indeed John. Dr. John Harvey, thirty-five-year-old, bachelor veterinarian. And what he had, made Molly delirious with joy.

"A kitten!" She dumped Lombard unceremoniously from her lap and jumped up. "Oh, please, can I hold it?"

John leaned down to her level, grinning broadly but

not yet ready to relinquish the tiny kitten held to the curve of his neck. "Who's this?" he asked Brooke.

"Dr. John, I'd like you to meet Molly Jackson, my new neighbor. Molly, Dr. John takes care of all my cats."

"How do you do?" Molly said gravely, but her gaze remained riveted on the cat. "May I—" She reached again for the kitten, her eagerness manifested in fingers trembling with anticipation.

Brooke restrained the child with a hand on her shoulder. "First Dr. John must meet your father," she said. "John, this is Garrett Jackson."

Garrett extended his hand. "How's it going, Dr. John?"

John laughed, then shook the proffered hand. "It's John Harvey," he said. "You're Miss Cora's heir, I presume?"

"That's right." Garrett looked watchful, neither friendly nor unfriendly. "Do you dump all your extra animals at Glennhaven?"

Brooke shot him an offended glance but John didn't bat an eye.

"Only the cats. Brooke sometimes helps me out until I can find new homes for those without them."

Molly piped up. "Is that kitten an orphan?"

John knelt before her, carefully dislodging the kitten from its haven. "What does a little girl like you know about a big word like orphan?" he asked gently.

"Because I am one," Molly said softly. Reaching out with a lightning-fast movement, she snatched the kitten from his hands and cuddled it to her chest.

Tears leapt to Brooke's eyes and she heard

Garrett's soft intake of breath but didn't dare to look at him. If Molly's words had hurt him, she didn't want to see it; if she did, she'd lose it for sure.

John glanced quickly at Garrett but didn't ask, for which she was grateful. He looked concerned when he spoke. "Brooke, can you give this little guy a home? He's a nice little cat, and healthy, too. One of my regulars found him wandering along the edge of the highway and since she lives in an apartment and already has three cats...well—" he shrugged "—you understand."

"Of course, John. The more, the merrier! Does he have a name?"

"No."

"Yes," Molly said.

Everyone looked at the girl except Brooke, who looked at Garrett. His expression revealed nothing.

Molly continued. "His name is Prince." She held the kitten with one hand, stroking with the other. Her face glowed with happiness. "Isn't he beautiful? Did you see his polka nuts?" She indicated patches of black on the kitten's white sides.

Brooke felt her eyes misting up again. She cleared her throat. "That's polka *dot*, sweetheart. And Prince is a wonderful name."

John chuckled. "Prince, it is."

"Hang on just a minute." Garrett hadn't said a word since the "orphan" comment, but now he came forward, in complete control, of course. "You can't have that cat, Molly."

"But—but—but—" Molly couldn't believe it; her entire body trembled.

"Garrett!" Brooke turned to him, unable to believe he could be so cruel. "You can't mean that."

"Be reasonable." He shoved one hand through his hair, a distracted gesture that didn't seem natural to him. "We've got two dogs living with us, remember? I think Baron would be okay with a cat, but you've seen Larry."

She certainly had. Her shoulders slumped but only for a moment. "Then can Prince be Molly's cat but live here?" she bargained. "You want me to spend time with her, right? She'll be here anyway, so what's the harm?"

His expression didn't soften. "Aren't you forgetting something else? At the end of the summer we'll be returning to Chicago and I can guarantee you we won't be taking a cat with us. What then?"

"Why don't we cross that bridge when we come to it?" she countered, stung by that reminder.

He hesitated, then drew a deep breath. "Okay, but remember that this was your idea when we *do* get to that bridge."

"I'll remember," she assured him. Turning to Molly, she said, "Congratulations! You're now the proud owner of a kitten. But he'll have to live here so the dogs don't hurt him."

Molly nodded, eyes aglow. "Can I stay here, too? Can I sleep with Prince? Can I feed him? Can I—"

"Whoa!" Garrett slipped an arm around her shoulders. "You'll see plenty of him, don't worry."

John turned toward the door, looking pleased. "In that case, I guess I've done my good deed for the day. I can head on home with a clear conscience."

Garrett's tone held a cautious edge. "Home to the wife and kiddies?"

John laughed. "I should be so lucky. Home to a frozen dinner and a stack of journals." He took Brooke's hand and squeezed it. "Thanks, hon. That's one animal I won't have to worry about anymore."

"Anytime, John." She walked with him to the door but her thoughts were on the man behind her. *When he left at the end of the summer—*

Nothing had changed, nothing at all.

The Fourth of July dawned hot and dry and bright, without a cloud in the sky. Despite trepidations that were very real, Brooke found herself looking forward to spending the day with Garrett and Molly. The truth was, she adored the little girl and—

She stopped short, in the act of filling Pookie's water dish. It would be far too easy to adore the father, as well. She kept forgetting what he was really after; what *was* he really after? One minute she thought it was her property and the next she thought it was *her*.

Maybe it was both. Well, he was only using her in any event—or trying to. He'd get neither and he might as well learn to live with it.

Once he appeared, though, she forgot all her reservations. He and Molly were dressed alike in jeans, long-sleeved shirts, despite the heat of the day, and good, strong hiking boots. So he wasn't a total neophyte when it came to tromping through the forest, she noted with approval.

He also carried two backpacks, presumably containing food. She'd taken him at his word and left all the details to him. While Molly rushed inside to say goodbye to the cats, Brooke faced him with a smile.

"Which backpack is mine?"

He hefted them, one in each hand. "This one," he said. "Turn around and I'll help you get into it."

Obediently she did as he directed, holding out her hands to accept the straps. He slid them over her arms and settled her pack into place.

"Feel all right?"

She rolled her shoulders forward, then back, checking. "Feels fine," she assured him.

"Not too heavy?"

"No."

"You're sure?"

He moved around to stand in front of her, his beautiful golden eyes filled with questions. All kinds of questions, surely not just an inquiry about a backpack. Brooke swallowed hard and tried to look away.

She couldn't do it.

It was as if he'd turned up the power on a magnetic force field. For a long moment their glances locked and then he reached for her.

She took a hasty step backward, breaking free of his magic. It was getting harder and harder to resist him, even knowing that in a month or two he'd be heading back to Chicago...to Dee-Dee and Caroline, no doubt, and who knew who else?

CHAPTER EIGHT

THEY stepped off into a magical Rocky Mountain day, the kind that grabs the imagination and never lets go. Before they'd gone a quarter mile, Brooke's spirits lightened, then took wing.

This was going to be a special day, she found herself thinking with a kind of hopeful expectation. But then, she reasoned, she loved these Rocky Mountains and never failed to respond to them.

Walking beside her, Garrett also seemed to tune in to the glories around him. Crossing grassy meadows with piney forests looming ahead, she noticed him looking around with an interest she'd never have expected.

Even Molly, although not happy to leave the cats behind, quickly captured the spirit of the adventure. While the two adults strode down well-defined paths, she ranged around them like a puppy happy to be set free.

Watching her, Brooke couldn't help smiling. "Molly's going to turn into a real mountain girl, if you don't watch her," she warned Garrett.

"Then I'll watch her—trust me." But he made that essentially negative statement with a smile that took away any potential sting.

They stopped at Seven-and-a-Half Mile Creek to take a breather.

Garrett looked around with clear curiosity. "But we haven't come seven-and-a-half miles yet," he reasoned, "probably less than two."

"Nobody ever told me seven-and-a-half miles from what," Brooke said with a smile. She eased the backpack straps across her shoulders, saw a flash of blue and turned to watch the flight of a butterfly. It landed on a silvery lupine flower. "Molly," she whispered urgently.

Molly glanced up from a close perusal of a pinecone resting on her palm.

Brooke pointed at the butterfly. "Come see."

Molly started forward but Brooke caught her arm. "Not so fast," she warned. "You'll scare him away. If we approach slowly...and make sure our shadows don't warn him that we're here..."

Setting words to action, she edged closer to the cluster of flowers.

"What is it?" Molly whispered, getting into the spirit of the thing.

"Just a plain blue butterfly," Brooke whispered back, "but isn't he pretty?"

"Oh-hh, yes!" Awe filled Molly's voice. "Can I—" And she reached for the butterfly.

Which fortunately frightened the critter. Taking flight, it easily evaded the little girl's reach.

"Make him come back," Molly wailed. "I want to play with him."

Brooke knelt beside the disappointed child. "But you don't want to hurt him," she said.

Molly looked confused. "I wouldn't hurt him."

"You would if you touched him. You'd kill him."

"I wouldn't!" Molly sounded highly insulted.

Brooke shook her head solemnly. "You would if you touched him. Butterflies are very delicate, honey. Even touching the wings makes all the pretty color come off and I know you wouldn't want to do that."

"N-no," the child admitted, not looking entirely convinced.

Garrett put a comforting hand on her shoulder. "Not to worry," he said cheerfully. "You can look all you want, you just can't touch." He gave Brooke a slightly challenging glance. "Which is true of a lot of things in this life, unfortunately."

Brooke laughed. The day was too beautiful, the air too clean, the occasion too appealing to take offense at his teasing. "Your father's right," she said lightly. "Shall we go on now? If we're lucky, we'll see a lot more interesting sights before we get to our picnic spot."

"Coward," Garrett said.

"Absolutely," she agreed, stifling a smile. "This way, everybody, and watch your step. The trail gets tricky from here on out."

And she led the way down the faint trail, deeper into a grove of trembling aspens.

Mrs. O'Hara had packed a lovely picnic. In addition to cold roast chicken, the backpacks revealed marinated mushrooms, her own homemade yeast rolls, a bag of melon balls, a nice bottle of white wine and a thermos of lemonade for Molly.

Brooke spread their oilcloth table covering on the edge of a flat-topped boulder which extended from the side of a hill out over a small valley. The view was spectacular, encompassing forest and meadow, mountain and valley. They ate in a companionable silence, broken only by Molly's occasional comment or the cry of some wild creature.

When the meal was finished, Molly climbed down off the rock and wandered a few feet away to examine a cluster of spiky paintbrush flowers, ranging from magenta to pale pink and red-orange. A sudden high-pitched whistle made her jump and utter a little shriek. A small furry body leapt from the cluster of flowers and disappeared into the tall grasses.

"What the hell!" Garrett crouched on the rock as if ready to go into action, the muscles of his arms corded.

"It's a squirrel," Molly cried, pointing.

"It's a marmot," Brooke corrected with a smile. "Don't worry, Garrett, he's gone. Molly scared him more than he scared her."

"Apparently." Garrett relaxed back to a seated position. "You seem to know a lot about the flora and fauna of this area, Brooke."

She shrugged. "Not really. I've picked up a little through the years but I'm no expert."

"Have you lived here long?"

"You mean with Miss Cora? About four years."

"I meant before that." He shifted so he could lay down on the rock on his side, bending one arm and resting his head on his palm. His long, denim-covered legs drew her attention but she forced herself to look away.

"I was born and grew up around Boulder," she

said after a moment. The question was a personal one and she found it slightly embarrassing to talk about herself to this man. He was so much more sophisticated than she; why would he care about her humble background?

"Your family lived here?"

She nodded but offered no further explanation.

He turned over onto his stomach, his chin very near her crossed legs. "Am I going to have to drag every syllable out of you?" he asked in a lazy, teasing tone. "I can, of course, but it would save us time if you'd just volunteer the information."

She knew he was right. She sighed. "That depends on what you want to know."

"The usual—family, interests, hobbies, all that sort of thing."

"It's not very interesting, really. I was born in Denver but my parents moved to Boulder when I was just a kid. My father owned a small gasoline station on the edge of town and my mother was a waitress."

"No kidding."

He sounded surprised. She supposed he'd never met the daughter of a waitress before. That thought brought a wry smile to her lips.

"Brothers or sisters?" he pressed.

"One sister, married with one child, living in Omaha. My parents moved to Florida after they both retired a couple of years ago, so I'm on my own."

"Do you miss them?" he asked, looking up at her with a gaze so penetrating she found it difficult to breathe. "Is that the reason my great-aunt became so important to you?"

"She was important to me from the moment I met her at Dr. John's office," Brooke said a bit defensively.

"Did you work there?"

"Yes." His determination to ferret out every corner of her life was beginning to make her anxious. "At one point, I'd wanted to be a veterinarian. That didn't work out, so I went to work for one. I was good with animals—"

"Except dogs," he reminded her.

She licked her lips. "Except dogs," she conceded. "Fortunately, John's practice is limited to cats, so that wasn't a concern." She couldn't resist making a *so-there* face at him.

He laughed and tiny lines radiated from the corners of those incredible golden eyes. This close to him, she could see into their depths, which made her wonder how anyone with such clear, honest eyes could be so...so duplicitous.

"Was your family close?" he asked.

"Not very. Miss Cora and I...needed each other, I guess. She became my family and I became hers." She met his steady gaze. "Do you mind?"

"Why should I mind?"

He said it carelessly but she sensed some deeper feeling beneath the quick, easy words. "It occurred to me that Miss Cora's real family might...I don't know, resent me? Might even think I was a fortune hunter, that I'd conned her into leaving me something I wasn't entitled to have."

"That...was mentioned."

"Really! Did you—do you actually think I'd do such a thing?"

"I did," he admitted slowly. "Now...it seems unlikely."

But not impossible, apparently. Brooke sat up straighter. Her thigh brushed his chin and she felt a jolt pass between them. Hastily she pulled back. "I'd think now that you know me—"

"I don't know you."

"I mean—"

"I know what you mean but I don't know *you*." He, too, sat up, and now it was their knees which brushed lightly. "What little I do know...is intriguing."

"Intriguing?" She didn't believe she'd ever been called intriguing in her life. It sent a little shiver of appreciation skittering down her backbone.

He nodded. Glancing around, he seemed to satisfy himself that Molly was nearby and safe before turning back to the woman seated beside him, holding her breath. With an easy, graceful movement, he caught her upper arms in a firm but not aggressive grip.

"I'd like to get to know you better, Brooke Hamilton...much better."

"I—I don't think...I mean, it doesn't seem...I can't—" She stammered to a halt, staring at him with stricken eyes. When he turned his full attention on her, she seemed to fall apart right on schedule.

His smile melted her bones. "You can if you want to. You're an adult, I'm an adult..."

He leaned toward her. He was going to kiss her, she just knew it. And heaven help her, she wanted it, and feared it, all at the same time. Her lips formed a single word. Don't! But that word was never said.

Instead, Molly's exclamation shattered the moment. "Look at that big bird, Gart!"

Both Garrett and Brooke turned automatically to follow the arm Molly extended toward the sky. Against a bright blue background, a hawk circled lazily, sleek confidence obviously in every line of its predator's body.

The raptor reminded Brooke of Garrett. And the dark clouds roiling up over the western mountains at the edges of a perfect sky reminded her that everything could change in a split second.

"We've got to go," she said, suddenly urgently. Pulling away from him, she stood up. "We're going to get a thunderstorm."

"You're kidding." But he, too, rose, looking at the sky.

"I'm not kidding." She began to gather up the remains of their picnic. "Let's get this stuff loaded and get out of here."

"You really think it'll rain?"

"I know it will."

"Want to bet?"

She glared at him, saw his knowing smile and groaned at her own naïveté. "Yes, I want to bet!" she challenged him. "I'll bet we're going to get wet before we get back to the house."

"Hmm." He considered. "Sounds like a sucker bet to me. I'll pass." He winked at her and turned away to call Molly to his side.

* * *

They ran the final fifty yards in pouring rain, although fortunately there'd been no claps of thunder or flashes of lightning. Garrett swung wide the wrought-iron gate, gesturing Molly through.

"Go on into the house," he called to her. "We'll be right behind you."

Molly waved and scampered away. Water streamed from her saturated hair and down her back; she was soaked to the bone. But so were the adults. In July heat, the rainwater seemed to hit the ground already steaming.

Brooke pushed wet hair away from her face, feeling exhilarated from the run...and perhaps from the company. "I'll go on home and get out of this wet stuff," she shouted over the pounding of the rain. "Thanks for a lovely—"

"Not quite yet."

Garrett stepped up to her, slipping one arm around her waist to bring her hips flat against his. He was as wet as she, his skin slick and his hair plastered against his head. There was something elemental and possessive about the way he looked at her.

She braced her hands against his biceps and pushed, which accomplished absolutely nothing. "What do you think you're doing?" she demanded.

"As if you didn't know," he said, and kissed her.

As she'd longed to be kissed ever since they'd started out on their Independence Day picnic. Sliding her arms around his waist beneath the backpack, she strained closer to him, the rain striking her upturned face and adding an extra dose of unreality to what was happening.

He lifted his head at last and the rain felt cool against her heated lips. He nuzzled her cheeks, her closed eyelids, and she sighed.

"Brooke," he murmured against her ear, "I've wanted to do this all day."

"Molly—"

"Yeah, but Molly's not here now. Why don't I walk you home...maybe come in for a...a..." The words were lost against the curve of her neck.

"D-drink?" she suggested, the word catching in her constricted throat. Clinging to him, she realized she was actually considering it.

"That, too." He stroked her hip with one hand while the other caressed her jawline. "Admit it, Brooke, I'm not the ogre you took me for."

"You're not?" She couldn't help reveling in the insanity of the moment: standing in the pouring rain in broad daylight, locked in the arms of a man who was practically a stranger. She had never done anything even remotely similar in her life. It went completely against her principles, but Garrett Jackson seemed to sweep those aside without effort.

"Well?" he urged, pressing urgent little kisses on her soft mouth. "Are you going to invite me home with you, sweetheart?"

She groaned. "I shouldn't..." And that was an understatement if there ever was one.

"But you want to. Why not go with the flow, for once?"

He took her mouth again in a kiss at the precise moment the first peal of thunder vibrated around them. For a moment, she didn't realize that nature had added stunning pyrotechnics to the power of a kiss that needed no such embellishment.

He pulled back slightly, laughing. "Is that thunder or just my heart?" he teased. "Come on, Brooke, let's get out of this."

"I'm still not sure...."

"I'm willing to bet you'll make the...appropriate decision." His grin was devilish.

"Garrett!" But he'd lightened the mood without diffusing it. Brooke felt every fiber of her being crying out for...him. Garrett Jackson. The man who'd already disrupted her life and would disrupt it more if she didn't take control.

So she took control. "Yes!" Stepping back, she grabbed his hand. "Let's go before—"

"Mr. Jackson! Mr. Jackson, are you out there?"

The voice belonged to Mrs. O'Hara. Brooke saw the woman's substantial figure standing at the kitchen door, peering out through the pouring rain.

"Damn!" Garrett muttered. He stepped forward as if to shield Brooke. "I'm here," he called. "What is it? I was just going to walk Brooke home."

"Telephone call!" Mrs. O'Hara shouted back. "For you."

"Take a message." He started to turn away, one hand going to Brooke's elbow to guide her back through the gate.

"But he says it's important!" Mrs. O'Hara had to shout to be heard through the storm.

"Oh, for—" He sounded annoyed. "Who is it, anyway?"

"It's the real estate agent," she called. "He says

he may have a buyer and wants to make an appointment to show the—''

Brooke yanked her elbow away and faced him. "A buyer! But I thought—"

"Don't jump to conclusions," he said quickly. He tried to touch her arm again but she bolted aside. "This is all just preliminary stuff, nothing for you to worry—"

"If you say it's nothing to worry my pretty little head about I'll—I'll *belt* you!" She held up a fist for emphasis.

"Well," he said defensively, "it's not, and you do have a pretty little head. The rest of you isn't bad, either."

His attempt to cajole her back into her previous receptive mood fell flat. A flash of painful understanding widened her eyes. "You're just trying to soften me up. Did you think that if you made love to me, I'd forget all my other objections?"

"It's nothing like that. Look, let's go on to your place and dry off a little so we can talk about this reasonably. You've got me all wrong—"

A clap of thunder seemed to shake the ground beneath her feet. With a gasp of shock, she took a step away from him, one hand flying to her throat. "I don't have anything to say to you," she cried, "except goodbye!"

Shrugging out of the backpack, she let it drop. Almost before it hit the ground, she was running down the path beneath the dripping trees, running for her life.

* * *

Disappointed, Garrett watched her go. Damn, he'd almost gotten through to her this time. She was as skittish as one of her cats but he'd made definite progress.

Until she realized he hadn't changed his mind or his plan, just his attack. He glanced over his shoulder at Mrs. O'Hara, still standing in the open doorway, and reminded himself that he shouldn't kill the messenger.

He didn't think he'd ever known a woman as natural as Brooke Hamilton. At first he'd thought her merely naive, and she was certainly that, but it was more...a certain willingness to take things, and people, at face value. And why not? It was always safe to take *her* at face value. If she had a devious bone in her body, he hadn't found it.

Of course, he'd just been prevented from looking too closely.

"Mr. Jackson!" Mrs. O'Hara interrupted his reverie. "You're going to catch your death, standing out there in all that rain! You come on in here, now, and talk to the man on the telephone while I fix you a nice hot cup of tea and lay out dry clothes. You come on in here now, you hear?"

Catch his death of cold? Garrett would have laughed if his current state of tension hadn't made a groan more appropriate. Brooke Hamilton was getting to him. The confirmed playboy was fighting for his existence.

Katy dropped by later, after the rain had stopped and the sun had come out once again. "Welcome to Colorado!" she exclaimed rhetorically, flinging her arms wide. "Where you get all four seasons, often in a single day."

Brooke, wrapped in a terry robe and with her hair still damp, sighed. "Come in and have a glass of lemonade, Katy. I could use the company."

"Have you been alone all day? I thought you were going on a picnic with that handsome hunk next door." She rolled her eyes appreciatively. Leaning over to pick up the white cat twined around her ankles, she followed her friend into the kitchen. "You guys get caught in the rain? It sure messed up the celebration in Boulder."

Brooke poured the tea. "The rain started just as we were finishing up. We got soaked walking back, though."

Katy's eyes narrowed. "Something else happened, from the looks of you."

"Don't be ridiculous." Brooke offered the glass.

"Did Garrett Jackson lay any moves on you?"

"Don't be ridiculous," Brooke said again.

"Did he?"

"Yes."

"I thought so." Katy cocked her head, her expression full of calculation. Suddenly she said, "Good!"

"What kind of friend are you? You're *glad*?"

Katy laughed. "Don't look so shocked. Your love life's been practically nonexistent since that mountain biker pedaled off into the sunset last year. Admit it, Brooke, a little summer romance is just what you need."

"That's what he thinks," Brooke said morosely.

Katy looked thoughtful. "And what do you think?" she asked. "I mean, *really*."

"I think..." What Brooke thought was that she was already in over her head where Garrett Jackson was concerned. If she let him finagle his way any closer— no, she dared not let him into her bed or her heart. "I think," she said more firmly, "that at the end of the summer he's going to sell out and go back to Chicago and I'll never see him again. So in answer to your question, no, I don't think a summer romance is what I need, at least not with *him*."

After knowing Garrett Jackson, maybe not with anyone, ever.

Grace Swann arrived while Katy and Brooke were finishing up their lemonade. Katy left while Grace baby-talked Pookie. When the elderly woman emerged, she found Brooke alone.

"So," she said in her usual brusque manner, "how's my Pookie been without me? Has he been eating?"

"He's been fine," Brooke said a bit distractedly. "In fact, I've let little Molly Jackson spend time with him and he seems quite taken with her."

Mrs. Swann frowned. "The child of that ungrateful man Cora left everything to?"

Uh-oh. She knew. "That's right," Brooke agreed.

"For a nickel, I'd bid on Glennhaven myself," the old lady said. "But then, what would I do with it? No, that's no good. You'll have to take it upon yourself to see Cora's wishes carried out, Brooke."

"Me? But I don't have any money. I couldn't possibly—"

"Who's talking money?" Mrs. Swann rolled her eyes expressively. "I'm talking sex appeal. Get into his good graces, convince him that he owes it to his auntie to carry out her wishes."

Brooke felt her cheeks blaze with embarrassment. "I couldn't possibly," she stammered. "Besides, it wouldn't work. He's not the kind of man who'd let a woman influence him...that way."

Mrs. Swann let out a loud guffaw. "*All* men are the kind who let women influence them, my dear. My goodness, Cora certainly did neglect your education." She turned toward the door, walking stiffly. "Pookie looks fine. Just keep on doing what you're doing."

"I will, Mrs. Swann." Brooke walked beside her.

"I wouldn't leave him anywhere except with you. He's a very valuable champion, you know, very valuable."

"I know, Mrs. Swann."

"And you better think about what I said, young lady." The old woman fixed her twinkling gaze on Brooke. "Work your womanly wiles on that young gentleman and I bet you'll be surprised by the outcome."

"I never bet, Mrs. Swann."

The old lady looked her young companion up and down. "And more's the pity!" she declared. "Brooke Hamilton, you've got to get out there and fight for what you want—and for what you don't want! And that's the truth."

Brooke watched the chauffeur-driven Bentley pull

slowly away, her thoughts in a whirl. At this point, she didn't know *what* she wanted, she only knew what she didn't want: to be left at the end of the summer with a broken heart, courtesy of the sexiest, most appealing man she'd ever met.

And tomorrow she was going to have to march right back into the lion's den....

CHAPTER NINE

BROOKE faced Garrett the next morning across the broad mahogany desk in Miss Cora's library. She'd lain awake practically all night, agonizing over what she might say to him. She had to say something; she simply couldn't face an entire summer with this kind of tension.

It was more than human flesh could stand—at least, more than *her* flesh could stand. She'd never been this attracted to any man before, which meant that Garrett Jackson was dangerous to her. She didn't want a summer romance, she wanted enduring love and a lasting commitment.

Sadly, Garrett didn't seem like the kind of man who'd ever take that kind of chance, regardless of his penchant for other kinds of risk-taking.

Which meant they had a few things to thrash out before they went on, she'd finally concluded. Thus she faced him in the bright light of day, tense and anxious. And there he sat in the big leather chair, a faint smile on his face while he waited for her to get on with it.

"We've got to get a few things straight," she said without even trying to ease into it.

His dark brows rose in a question. "Such as?"

She sucked in a deep breath. "Such as...how we're going to live together for the summer and—"

"Live together?" He made it sound like an intriguing possibility.

She felt herself flush. "You know what I mean. We're all here at Glennhaven and we've got certain things which need to be accomplished."

"Such as?" he asked again.

"Such as..." She gestured helplessly. "I promised Miss Cora I'd help get everything sorted and organized around here."

"All right. What else?"

"Well...I said I'd help you with Molly," she went on uncertainly. "Of course, if you want to hire a real nanny, it wouldn't hurt my feelings."

His smile was bland. "Not a chance. Molly's happier with you than she's been since...well, since her mother died." He picked up an antique crystal paperweight and balanced it on one palm. "You promised to help me with Molly. I thought your word was important to you."

She scowled. "It is. Isn't yours?"

His glance sharpened. "Of course."

She squared her shoulders and plunged to the heart of the matter. "Then give me your word that you'll stop...you won't..."

"Keep trying to sell this place?"

"No! That's not what I—" She realized what she was saying and caught herself. "Will you?"

"No."

"You won't sell?"

"I won't stop *trying* to sell. But obviously that's not what you were trying to say."

"Only because I didn't think there was a chance," she flared.

"And you were right," he agreed smoothly. "So, please, tell me what you *were* trying so hard to say."

"Oh. That." She chewed on her lower lip. "I don't want a summer romance, Garrett, so you can just stop...you know, stop..."

His smile sizzled. "Stop what, Brooke? Kissing you?"

She swallowed hard. "Th-that would be a good start."

"Stop putting my arms around you?"

"That, too."

"Stop trying to get you into my bed?"

"That's the big one!" She managed a shaky laugh.

"Don't you like me?" He stood up.

She bit off a groan. "That isn't the question."

"No?" He took a couple of steps around the desk. "Do you find me...repulsive?"

"Of course not. Just the opposite."

He rounded the corner of the desk; he was on her side of that puny obstacle now, and the gleam in his eyes was not what she wanted to see.

"What's the opposite of repulsive?" he mused. "Appealing...delightful..."

"No. Yes." She retreated a step. "You're confusing me, Garrett."

"I wouldn't want to do that." He kept coming. "I'd never do anything you didn't want me to do."

And he wasn't talking about "confusing her" when he said it, she realized. "That's what you say but not how you act," she blurted.

His grin turned wolfish. "Untrue! I'd only want you in my arms if you came of your own free will."

"Then it will never happen, so we have nothing more to discuss—on that subject, at least."

He started to respond but before he could, Molly skipped into the room with Larry the terrier at her side. "Look, everybody," she commanded. "Larry's got a trick."

Pulling back one arm, she let fly. Something small and bright streaked across the room—straight at Brooke.

With a yelp, Larry flew after it.

Brooke's heart leapt with surprise and fright. Without hesitation, she threw herself against Garrett's chest. His arms closed around her with a certainty that felt incredibly right.

"Larry!" he commanded. "Get away!"

Larry did—but first he grabbed an orange rubber ball that had come to rest between Brooke's feet. Then he slunk back to his small mistress.

Who looked at Brooke, still in Garrett's arms. Molly's eyes went wide, then filled with tears.

Garrett's face paled. "Molly, what is it?" he asked.

"My daddy used to hug my mommy a lot," she said in a choked voice, "but you never hug anybody, Gart."

Embarrassed by the girl's words, Brooke tried to pull away. To her surprise, he wouldn't let her go.

He spoke gently to Molly. "I hug *you*." He added a muttered, "When you'll let me," which the girl couldn't have possibly heard.

The confusion on Molly's face tore at Brooke's

heart. "Everybody needs a hug sometimes," Brooke said, sliding her arms around a surprised Garrett. She gave him a big hug and then withdrew before he could prevent it. "Would *you* like a hug, Molly?"

The little girl looked torn. Finally she said, "Not today, thank you." She turned back to the dog and made a stab at snapping her fingers. "Come, Larry—bad, Larry!"

She lured him from the room, scolding him with every step.

Embarrassed, Brooke sought escape. "I've got to get to work," she told Garrett uncomfortably. "There's a lot that needs to be—"

He cut her off sharply. "Why are you so terrified of dogs, Brooke? You practically threw yourself into my arms, as if you thought Larry was coming after you."

"At least I came of my own free will, just like you predicted."

"Don't joke about it. You were terrified. I want to know why."

"Let it go. It all happened a long time ago."

"But it obviously still bothers you—a lot."

She didn't want to talk about this, but a look at his determined expression told her that he wouldn't take no for an answer. "I was about eight, I guess." She began hesitantly. "A dog jumped a fence to get to me. I was just skipping along the sidewalk with my sister one minute and the next this—this brute was—"

"Easy." He didn't try to take her in his arms again, just touched the side of her face with gentle fingers.

His amber eyes offered encouragement. "What kind of dog was it?"

She sucked in a deep breath and went on in a voice that trembled. "Black, brown—I don't know. I don't think I really want to remember."

"How badly were you hurt?"

She shrugged away from his touch, in control of herself again. "I was in the hospital a couple of days. I have a few scars..."

"A few that can be seen and apparently some that can't. Didn't you say you were bitten twice?"

She managed a tense laugh. "About six months later, but that was just a simple nip of the fingers. It reinforced my feelings about dogs, though. I'm terrified of them, Garrett. I can't help it."

He cocked his head. "Yes, you can. You don't have to be best friends with them but there's no reason you have to walk around in a state of terror. Dogs are like people—there are a few bad apples but most of them are okay if you give them a chance. Take old Baron."

"You take him," Brooke said. "I don't want anything to do with him or that other one, either. Which reminds me—Gable's going crazy, not getting to come up to the big house with me. Is there any chance that at least while I'm working here, you could put the dogs outside so I can bring the cat along? I—I'd really appreciate it."

For a moment he seemed to be considering. Then he nodded. "I'll do it for *you*, Brooke, not for the convenience of some damned cat."

"Whatever. I appreciate it." She backed toward the door. "I'll get to work, then."

"I'll put Baron out and join you."

Still shaken, she nodded and left the room.

Garrett watched her go, realizing that he'd finally have to admit that between Brooke and Molly, he had troubles.

He'd tried so hard to protect Molly from his romantic adventures...which he suddenly realized had been fading away toward nothingness since he had willingly taken on the task of raising his small niece. Her reaction to finding Brooke in his arms made him wonder if he'd done the right thing, insulating her from outward displays of affection toward others.

And Brooke... She was struggling so hard to keep her distance, and failing miserably. She was his for the taking. All he had to do was decide if...or maybe that was more honestly stated as *when*.

But he had much to consider before making any moves on her, more than with any of his other...romantic conquests. Brooke was...different. Special. She deserved far more than the summer romance he'd been offering.

But Brooke wasn't his main concern, he reminded himself irritably. Of overriding importance was the well-being of the small person whose happiness depended solely upon him.

That same small person who had never called him father....

July passed in a blur of tension and work. Faithful to her own obligations, still Brooke refused to short-change her cats. Although her greatest desire was to finish her work at the big house so she could stop going there every day, she had other responsibilities.

One of them was Molly. The more time she spent with the little girl, the more Brooke's heart opened to the child, still fumbling toward some kind of closure to her parents' deaths. If Brooke could help her do that, she must.

And always, of course, there was Garrett. True to his word, he didn't press his attentions upon her. But he still looked at her as if she were a lollipop or an ice-cream cone, and she knew that all she had to do was crook her little finger....

Still, she assured herself, everything was going fine.

Or at least, as fine as she had any reason to expect, with the little matter of Glennhaven and its fate still in limbo.

"Brooke Hamilton!"

Garrett's roar penetrated walls to reach her in the sitting room of Miss Cora's suite, where she was sorting handkerchiefs and scarves taken from an overflowing chiffonier. Beside her, Molly looked up in alarm.

"Brooke! Come in here—now!"

Molly's eyes widened. "Uh-oh!" she exclaimed. "Gart sounds mad. We better go."

"*I* better go." She didn't know what was up but thought it better to face him without Molly for a witness. She reached for the child too late, for Molly scooted away and out the door.

Brooke followed at a run, entering the hallway just in time to see Molly disappear through Garrett's open doorway. Racing inside, she stopped short at the sight that met her eyes.

Gable sat in the middle of Garrett's bed, licking his paws. He was surrounded by the tattered remnants of a sweater...Garrett's sweater...Garrett's *cashmere* sweater. And the obnoxious creature didn't even have the good grace to look ashamed of himself!

Brooke's horrified gaze swung from the unrepentant feline to the sweater's owner, who looked mad enough to grab Gable and strangle him. The tension thickened; Brooke held her breath.

And then Molly began to giggle. She put one hand over her mouth but couldn't hold back her glee. Garrett swung on her, his fury palpable but quickly replaced by puzzlement.

Molly pointed. "Gart, remember you told me about the cat that swallowed the canary?"

"Yes, but what's that go to do with anything?"

Molly laughed harder. "Gable looks like the cat that swallowed the sweater. He's got strings stuck in his teeth!"

And he did—strands of yarn and bits of knitted fabric trailing down his chin. For a moment, Garrett stared at the cat and then he began to smile...chuckle...finally bursting into a full-fledged roar of laughter.

Sitting on the side of the bed, he held out his arms and Molly walked into them without hesitation; the two laughed together. Relieved, Brooke watched for a moment, then turned quietly and slipped out the door. She didn't belong here; this was a moment for the two to share alone. She'd apologize to Garrett later and offer to replace the sweater.

But later, he shrugged off that suggestion with a smile. "It's worth a dozen sweaters to have Molly give me a hug," he said. "It even makes me feel a little more charitable toward old Gable."

Which made Brooke feel more charitable toward not-so-old Garrett. A man who cared so much for a child, and who could give others—even cats—the benefit of the doubt, couldn't be all bad.

She felt herself softening even more toward him. "At least let me do something to make amends," she insisted. "Anything—"

"Anything?" That light in his amber eyes warned her.

"Except that!" But she was laughing when she said it. "I'm not going to serve you breakfast in bed so you may as well forget it."

"You treat me worse than you treat your cats," he complained mournfully.

"My cats have never tried to take advantage of me," she snapped.

"That you know of," he added, winking at her. "Okay, I know when I'm licked. Then how about...how about coming over for a swim tonight? You and Molly and me—I'll barbecue."

She shook her head. "Sorry."

"But—"

"Hey, I'm the one who lost the bet," she reminded him lightly, "not you. I'm ready to pay up—" She raised one brow. "Within reason. You and Molly come to my house for dinner tonight, okay? I'm not much with barbecue but I'm pretty good with enchiladas and Spanish rice.''

''It's a date.'' He stuck out his hand as if to shake on it.

She shoved her own hand behind her back. ''Not a date, just a...an appointment? No, a dinner engagement, that's all.''

''It's a date, don't kid yourself.''

Before she knew what he was doing—or at least admitted it to herself, he swept her into his arms. The kiss he gave her was filled with a kind of yearning that had never been there before, and against which she found she had no defense.

Without thought, she lifted her arms and slipped them around his neck, kissing him back. When he leaned down and lifted her in his arms she didn't protest, just pressed her cheek against the curve of his throat and tried to catch her breath.

But when he deposited her on Miss Cora's big canopied bed, she groaned and rolled away. ''Stop, Garrett!''

He did, with one knee already on the bed. He looked at her as if he couldn't believe it. ''You're kidding,'' he said flatly.

She shook her head miserably, then buried her flaming face in her hands. ''I'm not,'' she said, her voice muffled. ''I'm not ready to be just another notch on your bedpost.''

''Another—'' He sounded stunned. ''Is that what you think is going on here?''

She forced herself to lower her hands and look at

him. "What else? Summer romance, remember? I told you all along I wasn't ready for that and I'm still not. If that's all you want from me—"

"I...don't think it is."

"That's right, I almost forgot. You're also after my home."

He pushed himself off the bed and stood up, shoving his hair away from his face with both hands. He didn't look angry, just perplexed. "Damn, Brooke," he said, "you've got a one-track mind."

She looked at him incredulously. "Look who's talking. As far as my land goes—"

"Forget the damned land!"

She stared at him. "But isn't that what this is all about?"

"Hell, at this point I don't even *know* what this is all about." He sucked in a deep breath. "Forgive my disappointment, but I really thought—"

What had he thought? *What had he thought?*

"Never mind that," he went on brusquely. "Is six all right?"

"All right for what?"

"Dinner, what else?"

"Oh...yes, it's fine, but are you sure you still want to come after what just happened?"

He gave her an enigmatic glance over one shoulder. "Nothing happened—with you, nothing ever happens. But, yeah, I'm sure." His eyes narrowed. "You wouldn't be trying to get out of it, would you?"

"Not...exactly. It's just that..." Just that what? That she couldn't be in the same room with him without wanting to be in his arms? That when she was in his arms she wanted to be in his bed? That if she ever surrendered to that desire she'd spend the rest of her life trying to get over it?

She gave in helplessly. "I'll see you at six, then."

"At six."

She watched him walk out of the room, then sat there staring at the door until tears welled in her eyes to blur its outline. Giving up, she rested her cheek against the satin coverlet and let the tears fall unchecked. She hadn't known she'd had so many tears to shed.

Feeling as if her heart were breaking, she felt something wet and warm touch her temple. Her breath caught in her throat and she froze. What in the—

Holding herself very, very still, she opened her eyes just a crack, prepared to scream or run or fight off whatever had penetrated this mist of misery. It was something big and hairy and—

Baron whined deep in his throat and licked her hand. She had never seen such sympathy in the eyes of another living creature, or maybe she just needed compassion and thought it was there. But she couldn't mistake the big dog's gentle concern. With a strangled cry, she slid her arms around his neck and buried her face in his rough coat.

Sometimes, she thought incoherently, we have to take sympathy where we can get it—even from a dog.

She felt much better afterward. It seemed as if she'd been holding her emotions in check forever, and it was good to just let go.

It also felt good to realize she'd found a friend in

Baron. Not that she'd let him change her mind about dogs in general; for example, she still had an aversion to that awful little Larry. But she was ready to admit that Baron was a special case.

That was the first step, at least.

Fortunately, she was able to slip out of the house without having to face anyone and explain her red eyes and flushed face. Back in her own home, she hurried to care for the cats before beginning dinner preparations. Each had to have his special food, his special playtime, his special attention.

All of which she provided, even if automatically. It seemed incredible but thoughts of Garrett were actually intruding upon the most important aspect of her life, her cats.

What did that say about her...about him...about her hopes for a happy future?

By the time the Jacksons arrived at six o'clock, everything was in good order. Brooke greeted them at the door, showered and refreshed. Dinner was well under way and her emotions were well under control.

Molly looked around, rubbing her small hands together in anticipation. Gable and Lombard and Deadeye Dick and Prince were in the sitting room but Molly wanted more.

"Can Pookie play, too?" she asked.

Brooke frowned. "I'm not sure that's such a good idea. Pookie's such a valuable animal...."

Molly's lower lip trembled and Brooke gave in without so much as a fight. "Oh, what the heck! He likes you so much, and he misses Mrs. Swann so much—sure, I'll bring him out. But you've got to promise to help me keep a really close eye on him. If anything happened to him—'' She gave an exaggerated shudder and went to fetch the big Maine coon cat.

With Molly settled with the cats, Brooke went about final dinner preparations, maintaining a determined good cheer. Garrett looked a little puzzled, a little thoughtful, but willing to go along.

They ate enchiladas and tacos and Spanish rice outdoors on the deck, shaded by pine trees and caressed by a gentle east wind. Conversation was light and superficial, and Brooke found herself wondering if he was also thinking about what had passed between them a few hours earlier.

He was thinking about *something*. He seemed distracted, frequently glancing at his watch as if eager to make his getaway.

Well, that was fine with her! She'd only invited him because she thought she had to. While he took Molly inside to wash her face after dinner, Brooke began to clear the table. She'd tell him he'd done his duty and was free to go, she decided. Just as soon as he returned—

The sound of an automobile approaching from the main road surprised her. Nobody wandered in here by mistake. Since she wasn't expecting anyone, it must be a visitor for Garrett.

Standing on the deck at the side of the house nearest the road, she shaded her eyes with one hand and watched the car, a large and shiny sedan, approach and slow to a stop. The passenger window lowered with a soft whir and the driver, a middle-aged man wearing a suit, leaned across the front seat to speak.

"I'm looking for Garrett Jackson. Would you happen to know where I might find him?"

She gestured. "He's inside."

"In that case—" The man killed the engine and climbed out, coming around the car to join her. "I'm Mike Pritchard." He stuck out his hand.

"Brooke Hamilton." She slipped her hand into his for a quick, firm shake.

"Ms. Hamilton—of course."

That surprised her. "Have we met?"

He grinned. "No, but I know all about you. I'm hoping you've used your woman's prerogative to change your mind."

It still wasn't registering. "About?"

He looked surprised. "About selling your land to Mr. Jackson. He's told me of your reluctance, and now having seen the place, I can certainly empathize. But I'm sure I can find you something equally suitable."

"Mr. Pritchard, hold on!" She stared at him. "Are you telling me that you're a...a real estate agent?"

"Why, yes, of course. You didn't know?"

"How would I know?" She struggled to come to grips with the undeniable fact that Garrett hadn't changed his mind at all.

"I just assumed—"

"*Too much*, Mr. Pritchard." The voice—Garrett's voice—slashed through the man's words. "You've assumed way too much."

"Mr. Jackson, I can assure you—"

"I told you eight-thirty at the main house."

"But my news is so good—"

"I don't care if your news is—" Garrett bit off his sharp words. He added in a more controlled tone, "I had news for *you*, but you've come at an inopportune moment."

The real estate agent retreated toward his car. "I'm beginning to sense that, Mr. Jackson. But I thought you'd want to know that your counteroffer has been accepted, on the condition that Ms. Hamilton's land is part of the package."

"My land?" Brooke felt as if someone had just stolen her Christmas stocking. "Garrett, how could you?"

"We'll talk about this later, Brooke." His voice was as grim as his expression.

"I've got nothing to say to you, now or ever!" She whirled away.

"Brooke—"

"Mr. Jackson," the real estate agent interrupted, "I tried to call but the phone lines must be—"

"Get out!" Garrett's rage erupted. "Get out of here before I throw you out!"

He got. Brooke heard his hasty footsteps, then the roar of the car engine. She didn't care. All she knew was that Garrett had betrayed her, going against Miss Cora's wishes in the bargain.

His hands closed over her shoulders and she shivered but wouldn't face him.

"Brooke, you know I can't sell your land if you won't let me," he said. "It isn't mine. But the rest of

Glennhaven *is*. That agent was just trying to put together the most valuable package.''

''You promised you'd reconsider.''

''I have,'' he said impatiently. ''I've been over this a thousand times. If you'll just listen to me, I think I might be able to—''

''What? Convince me that you're doing the right thing? I don't think so.'' A shiver of despair shook her. ''We have nothing further to say to each other,'' she concluded in a choked voice.

''Of course we do.'' He pulled her back until her shoulder blades pressed against his chest. ''I'm trying to tell you that I've made up my mind to—''

''Don't tell me *anything*, Garrett.'' She dared not listen to him or she'd be lost, even now. ''Just get out!''

''You don't mean that, Brooke.''

''I do! You never intended to abide by the terms of the will. You've just been trying to seduce me and I—I never want to see you again.''

His hands fell away from her shoulders. ''Don't do this. You make it sound as if the only thing at stake here is real estate. I want to make you understand—''

''I do understand,'' she cried. ''This *is* about real estate. You think I have no right to stand in the way because I'm nothing but a fortune hunter who took advantage of a lonely old woman.''

''I haven't thought that for quite a long time.'' His expression hardened. ''You're being unreasonable. I'm not used to taking orders and I don't think I like it. Understand that if you send me away now without listening to me, I won't be back. Are you certain that's the way you want this to end?''

''I'm not certain of anything,'' she said with a bitter little laugh, ''except that I feel like a fool.''

Another long silence. Then he said, ''I guess this comes down to real estate after all. I'll go get Molly.''

After he'd gone into the house, she stood trying to hold herself together until he was gone. Time seemed to stand still…and then she heard his rapid footsteps on the deck and forced herself to turn.

He looked—shocked, maybe even frightened.

''Garrett, what is it?'' She took a step toward him. ''What's happened?''

''It's Molly,'' he said. ''Brooke, she's gone and so is that damned cat!''

CHAPTER TEN

"THAT damned cat" was Pookie, a realization that barely registered with Brooke. "Gone?" she repeated. "What do you mean, Molly's gone? Gone where?"

"Back to the mansion, I hope." He glanced up the path, his anxious expression betraying his concern.

Brooke's heart slowed its wild beating as reason reasserted itself. "Why do you look so worried, Garrett? I'm sure that's where she must be. It's not like her to just take off without asking permission, but I'm sure—"

"That's what I thought until I found this near an open window," he interrupted. "That open window." A ribbon fluttered from his fingers as he pointed toward the window overlooking the deck where they'd just spoken to the real estate agent before tearing into each other.

"Oh, no!" She stared at him in horror. "You don't suppose she heard us?"

"How could she help it? We weren't exactly being quiet." He crushed the bit of satin between his fingers. "I'm sure you're right, though. There's nothing to worry about." He spoke without noticeable sincerity. "She's just gone back home."

"Taking Pookie with her?" Brooke whispered. "Oh, Garrett, that's not like her at all. She knows the cats aren't supposed to leave my house."

169

"Especially that one," he agreed glumly. "If anything happens to that cat—" He didn't finish the sentence, just turned and strode away.

He didn't need to finish; Brooke knew. Pookie was the most valuable, not to mention one of the most beloved, cats in all of Catty-Corner. If anything happened to him she'd have to change the name of her business to Cat-Astrophe!

Even so, the cat was just a peripheral worry, his significance paling beside the disappearance of Molly. Brooke hurried after Garrett. "I'll bet we find her in her own room and Pookie with her," she panted.

"That's one bet I hope you win," he said grimly.

But she didn't win it, for there wasn't a sign of either girl or cat in the mansion. Although Garrett and Brooke ran through every hallway and opened every door, they came up empty.

Meeting in the front entryway, Brooke saw her own fear mirrored in Garrett's expression. She longed to throw herself into his arms, both to comfort and to offer comfort, but knew she had no right after all that had happened.

And especially not after she'd so recently told him she never wanted to see him again. In the face of this new and developing horror, the fate of Glennhaven seemed insignificant at most.

He must have seen her fear for he started to reach out to her, then pulled back. "We'll find her," he promised, "and that damned cat, too. How far could they have gone?"

He spoke with fresh confidence, as if he meant it

this time. The possibility that he did filled her with renewed hope.

"You're right. We're being silly." She sucked in a deep breath and gave him a bright smile. "Let's look around outside. She might be in the yard with the dogs."

Only she wasn't. Baron, stretched out in the shade under a tree, looked confused by so much activity, while Larry followed along, yipping constantly. As always, the little dog sent a cold shaft of fear through Brooke. This time she shoved it down; she had no time for that.

"Now what?" she asked anxiously. "We've looked everywhere."

"We've looked in the obvious, but not everywhere." His glance rose to touch on the dark forest at the edge of the meadow just beyond the manicured lawns and gardens of Glennhaven. "Do you suppose..."

"Oh, God, no! You don't think she'd go into the forest, do you?"

"You wouldn't think so, but she did enjoy our picnic the other day. I guess it all depends on why she took off in the first place."

Their glances locked and Brooke wondered if his thoughts were as guilty as hers. They shouldn't have been fighting, but if they were going to fight, it shouldn't have been within the hearing of a child as sensitive as Molly.

"I'm sorry," she said miserably. "This is all my fault."

His beautiful golden eyes narrowed. "Why would you think that?"

"You know why," she said. "I shouldn't have fought with you. What you do with your property isn't any of my business and never was."

"Hey," he said with a shrug, "you're entitled to your opinion."

"Am I?" She felt like crying. "Garrett, if—*when* we find Molly safe and sound, I'll *give* you my inheritance and you can do any darned thing with it you want."

He gave her a wary smile. "Bet you change your mind when the time comes," he predicted.

"Bet I don't," she retorted.

"What're the stakes?" He was getting into the spirit of the thing. "Breakfast in bed?"

"Yes! Yes, yes, yes!" She clenched her hands together to keep from grabbing him. "Garrett, I didn't mean what I said back there—not most of it, anyway."

And at last she gave in and did what she'd been longing to do: threw herself into his arms and pressed her cheek beneath the curve of his chin to draw comfort from his touch. Without hesitation, he wrapped her in his arms and they stood there together, sharing their fears.

And that was when she admitted something to herself that she'd been fighting almost since the day she met him.

She loved this man with all her heart.

Molly wasn't in the meadows; she wasn't anywhere near the tennis courts or the storage buildings or the old carriage house. Standing at the edge of the trees where the trail curved out of sight, Brooke turned to Garrett with renewed anguish.

"Please tell me you don't think she's in there!"

He looked past her into the darkening trees. Behind them, in the yard of the big house, Larry's excited yaps disturbed the hush. At eight o'clock at night, they didn't have much daylight left.

"I wish I could," he said finally, "but I'm afraid she may be. We've looked just about everywhere else. Brooke, I think it may be time for us to call for help."

"You mean, the police?" The thought was abhorrent to her, almost like giving up. "Do we have to?"

"I think we do."

She had another horrible thought. "What if the telephone still isn't working? That real estate agent said he'd tried to call you and—"

His groan interrupted her. "That's right, he did. Damn, Brooke, we're running out of options here."

He thrust his hand through his hair and she saw the ribbon flutter between his fingers.

He glanced back toward the house, his face twisting into a grimace of frustration. "If that damned dog doesn't quit barking, I swear—"

"Garrett, that's it!" She gripped his elbow in her excitement.

"What's it?" He frowned at her as if she'd lost her mind.

"Larry! Maybe Larry can find her."

He understood at once. "Damn! You could be right. Larry's a terrier and they're hunting dogs, or were once upon a time. It's sure worth a try. Let's go!''

Grabbing her hand, he set off across the meadow at a run, pulling her along behind him. Whatever happened, he obviously felt as she did on one critical point: they were in this together. The only thing that mattered now was finding Molly and bringing her back home, safe and sound.

While Brooke tried the telephone, Garrett rounded up the dogs. When she came out of the house shaking her head in disappointment, he had both animals leashed and ready to go.

"Phone's dead, huh?"

"I'm afraid so. We're on our own, Garrett."

His quick, excited smile buoyed her spirits.

"Don't worry, Brooke. This is going to work. Old Larry's gonna come through for us this time."

"Oh, God, I hope so," she said. "If that miserable hound saves the day, I'll...I'll make friends with him if it kills me."

Garrett's expression was warmly approving. "Then get ready to make the ultimate sacrifice, because we're on our way."

And they were, out the gate and back to Brooke's house where they led the dogs to the window where Garrett had found the ribbon. Kneeling, he offered them the bit of blue to sniff and examine. Then he unleashed both animals, sat back on his heels and said in a clear, confident voice, "Find Molly! Find Molly and it's sirloin steak for dinner!"

* * *

Brooke and Garrett charged through the trees on the trail of a yapping Larry and a calm Baron. The dogs ranged on either side of the faintly defined track, noses to the ground and, at least in the terrier's case, tail waving jauntily. Larry was obviously enjoying the hunt.

Brooke found she didn't have time to worry as she challenged herself to keep up with the dogs and the man. Breathless and excited and hopeful, she clung stubbornly to their heels, determined to be with them when they found—

They *had* to find Molly, and Pookie, too. They just had to. Brooke glanced up at a dark sky. Twilight was nearly gone and full darkness would settle over them in a matter of minutes. Dare they continue to thrash through the wilderness under those conditions?

True, she'd grabbed a flashlight at her house, but that was a puny weapon against such vastness. The poor little girl must be—

Brooke stumbled and went to her knees. She knew a moment of panic; Garrett was so concentrated on the search that he wouldn't even know she was no longer behind him.

But before this new worry could take hold, strong hands lifted her and set her back on her feet. He was just a shadow in the darkness but he was there, her hero.

Her love.

That knowledge was still so new that it slammed into her, taking her breath away. She must have gasped for he tightened his grip with quick concern.

"Are you hurt?" His tone was anxious.

"No, no. I'm—'' Stunned, shocked, exhilarated. In love. "I'm sorry. Let's go on."

He nodded and released her. A sudden change in the pitch of Larry's incessant yipping alerted them both of some change in the status of the search.

He reached for the flashlight she still clutched in her hand. "They've found something," he said in a tone remarkable only in its neutrality. "Stay behind me, Brooke."

He wanted to protect her from whatever they might discover. For the first time she realized that he wasn't as sure of a successful outcome as he'd led her to believe. He'd been trying to keep her spirits up—and she loved him for that and for so much more.

Slipping a finger through one of his belt loops, she blundered after him in the dark, content to let him show her the way.

They found a very frightened little girl nestled in the exposed roots of a tree a few feet off the trail, where they could easily have passed it in the dark without the dogs to alert them. The revelations in the beam of the flashlight struck Brooke all at once: the tear tracks on Molly's cheeks, her hair straggling around her shoulders, the dirt on her T-shirt and the disheveled condition of the cat clutched in her arms.

And her joy at seeing them. She looked up into the blinding light and her lips formed a singled word: "D-daddy?"

Garrett groaned and dropped to his knees, inadvertently losing the flashlight in the process. While he swept Molly into his arms, Brooke picked up the flashlight, illuminating the scene more discreetly than he had done.

With a lump in her throat, she watched Garrett embrace the girl, dreading the moment when Molly would realize it was her uncle, not her father, who held her. When Molly lifted her face from his shoulder, Brooke knew what was coming—and dreaded it, for his sake.

The little girl smiled and reached out to touch his cheek gently. She said, in a very clear, young voice, "Daddy! I knew you'd save me!"

Brooke could have wept with joy.

Garrett carried Molly back to the house, holding her as tenderly as if she were his heart. Brooke walked beside them, carrying Pookie, who was less than pleased with this turn of events. After spending even a little time wild and free in the forest, he apparently had decided he liked it and would just as soon stay.

That would have lasted until mealtime, she figured, hanging on to the big cat fiercely. Getting him back in one piece was part of the miracle of finding Molly in the same condition. *Thank you, God!* she whispered, looking up into the fathomless expanse of starry sky. *Thank you.*

Back at the mansion, the dogs were released into the yard with a promise of steak dinners to come. Then Garrett carried Molly upstairs to her own bathroom, where she was summarily deposited in a tub of warm water.

Once the dirt washed away, they found the girl had a few scratches and minor bruises but was otherwise unharmed. When she was dried with fluffy towels and wrapped in her own pink and frilly nightgown, Garrett sat down on the rocking chair next to her canopied bed and pulled her onto his lap.

"Now, Molly, we've got to talk about what happened," he said gently.

Taking that as her cue, Brooke edged toward the door, Pookie clasped against her chest. "Maybe I should go see to—"

"Don't move!" Garrett fixed her with a commanding gaze. "You're part of this. I want you to stay."

"Are you sure?" She glanced significantly at Molly. "I wouldn't want to intrude."

His expression remained unyielding so she sat on a padded satin bench at the foot of the bed, easing the cat down beside her. The big creature settled in with a sigh. He needed attention as badly as Molly had; he looked ragged and dirty, but satisfied.

Throughout all this, Molly kept her gaze on Garrett's face. He gave Brooke an enigmatic nod before turning back to his child.

"Tell us what happened, Molly."

"What happened?" She screwed up her face as if trying to fathom his meaning.

"Why did you run away?" he continued patiently.

She looked astonished. "I didn't run away, Daddy."

A shiver moved Garrett's broad shoulders. This time there could be no mistake; she had deliberately called him by the name he'd longed to earn.

He cleared his throat. "Then why—"

"*Pookie* ran away," she explained. "When I

opened the door he ran out on accident." She cast an anxious glance at Brooke. "You and Ms. Brooke would be mad at me if he got lost so I ran after him."

Brooke leaned forward. "Oh, Molly, I wouldn't have been mad at you."

"You were mad at Daddy," she said with unerring reason, "and he didn't do anything wrong like I did."

Garrett and Brooke exchanged significant glances, hers filled with guilt. Then he said to Molly, "You heard us arguing then."

She nodded. "Yelling. Mama and my first daddy yelled sometimes, but then they kissed and made up. Did you and Ms. Brooke do that?"

"Not yet," Garrett said grimly. "So you heard us yelling and you wanted to tell us to kiss and make up. But then Pookie ran out the door and you went after him. Is that how it happened?"

Molly nodded. "I couldn't catch him," she said, her brow wrinkling. "I kept chasing him and chasing him..." She frowned at the memory. "Then it started to get dark but I didn't know how to get home again." Tears squeezed from the corners of her exhausted eyes. "I—I think I saw a monster."

Garrett hugged her fiercely against his chest. "I'll bet it was just a shadow. I don't think Pookie and Larry would let any monsters live at Glennhaven, do you?"

"I don't know," she said, unconvinced. "I hope...not." She was wilting, sinking deeper into her father's embrace. Her lips parted in an enormous yawn. "Do you still love me, Daddy?" Her eyelids drifted closed.

"I'll love you until the day I die, no matter what."

"I love you...too. And Ms. Brooke..."

She was asleep almost before the final word was uttered. Quietly he rose and deposited her on her bed, pulling the flower-strewn sheet up to her shoulders. Smoothing damp hair away from her forehead, he leaned down to kiss her.

Brooke lost it. Blinded by tears, she slipped out the door and ran.

Garrett caught up with her on the front porch, grabbing her by the waist and swinging her around. Pookie sprang from her arms and stood glaring up at them indignantly. Before she could grab the cat again, she was being grabbed herself, grabbed and pulled into a pair of strong arms.

"Where the hell do you think you're going?" he demanded, his voice gritty.

"Home," she said. "Tomorrow I'll start looking for someplace to relocate Catty-Corner."

"What the hell for?" he asked, obviously astonished by her announcement.

"You know why." She put her hands on his arms and tried to push him away.

"No, I don't."

"Yes, you do! I said if we found her safe and sound, you could have my property. We did and you can. Call Mr.— Mr. Whatever-his-name-was and tell him to make the deal."

"Don't be ridiculous." He pressed her hard against his body, chest to knee. "You're not going anywhere."

"You can't tell me what to do." Words were cheap. They'd been through such a traumatic experience tonight that she felt completely open and vulnerable to her newly recognized love for him. Still, she wouldn't hug him back; she wouldn't!

She kept telling herself that, even as her traitorous arms crept around his lean waist, even when she leaned her cheek against his shoulder with a sigh.

"I don't want your land," he murmured, nuzzling her temple. "Not anymore, anyway."

She swallowed hard. "What *do* you want, then?"

"I want to kiss and make up, just like Molly suggested."

"Oh, Garrett, don't tease. I know what you really want and it's a lot more than a kiss."

"All right, Brooke, in your infinite wisdom, tell me what it is I want."

"You've never made a secret of it. You want my land and you want me, or at least, you did." She swallowed hard, then went on bravely. "I guess...I guess a summer romance *is* better than no romance at all."

His eyes, sparkling in the faint porch light, widened. "Surely you don't mean..."

"I think...I do!" When she nodded for emphasis, her cheek caressed his throat above his V-necked shirt. "I don't want to fight you anymore," she admitted. "Life's too uncertain. If you want a summer romance, you can have one—no questions asked, no conditions. I'll even concede this is your house and you can do anything you want with it, including sell it, and I won't say another word on the subject."

"Is that so."

She couldn't read a thing in his voice. "You are going to sell it, right?"

"Wrong. I intended to tell Pritchard tonight to take it off the market, but you wouldn't give me a chance to explain that."

Her heart leapt…but perhaps not with joy. "Then you're going to turn it into a cat shelter?" If he did, he'd still be gone, out of her life just as he'd intended from the first.

"No," he said again.

She frowned. "I thought those were your only two choices."

"There's one more." Leaning down, he dropped a swift, hard kiss on her lips. "I've decided to stay here, me and Molly, at least for the time being."

"Y-you are?" She could hardly believe her good fortune, or the joy his announcement brought with it. "Why, Garrett? I really don't understand."

His grin unfolded slowly. "It took a while but I finally realized there's nothing waiting for me in Chicago that I can't do without. I decided I had to hang around here in hopes of getting my breakfast in bed."

"Had to?"

He stroked her back. "*Had to*. Brooke…"

"Yes, Garrett?" She could barely breathe.

He sighed. "I didn't know it would be this hard."

"*What* would?"

"Nothing much. I'm just trying to work up the…courage…"

"Courage? You?"

"Don't laugh." He held her away so he could look into her eyes. "It takes courage when you're thirty-two years old and your intentions are honorable for the first time in your life."

Her knees went weak. "How honorable?"

"I-love-you-truly, church-and-wedding-ring honest. I've never told a woman I loved her before so I'm not doing too good a job of this, but I'm trying to say it to you now."

"That you love me? Oh, Garrett!"

He enfolded her in his embrace. "Don't keep me in suspense. What do you say, Brooke? Care to make it legal?"

"I—yikes!"

At the probing exploration of her ankle by something wet and cold, she gave a little shriek and bounded out of his arms. Looking down, she saw Larry standing there, staring up at her with bewilderment on his doggy face. His tail gave a tentative wag. For the first time since she'd met him, he wasn't yapping his fool head off.

Garrett cupped her chin in his hand and turned her face toward his. "Ignore the dog and say what I want to hear," he pleaded.

"I will," she promised, "but first I owe our furry friend an apology."

Dropping to her knees, she threw her arms around Larry's neck. Behind her she heard Garrett mutter, "If I didn't love you, I'd think you were crazy."

Giggling in the hallway awakened Brooke. Coming to full consciousness slowly, she took stock of her surroundings.

She lay on satin sheets in the big bedroom which had been Miss Cora's but was now hers...hers and her new husband's. They'd returned from their November honeymoon quite late the night before and hadn't even had a chance to see Molly yet.

Everything had worked out beautifully. Molly, flower girl at their wedding, had reluctantly stayed behind with Mrs. O'Hara to await her parents' return from the honeymoon. Katy had been thrilled to move into the gatehouse and take over the running of Catty-Corner on an indefinite basis.

All truly was well that ended well.

Garrett stirred beside her now, reaching for her. He pressed a kiss on her bare shoulder, slid a hand beneath the covers to stroke her hip before his magnificent golden eyes had even opened. "I love you," he murmured. "Brooke?"

"I love you, too," she said, which was the naked truth. She captured his roving hand in hers. "But I think you'd better hold off on proving it. Something's going on out in the hall. I think we're about to have company."

"Company?" He roused up in the bed, his black hair a becoming tangle. "I don't want company. I want—"

"Surprise!"

The door burst open and Molly stood there, holding a silver tray in her little hands. "Mrs. O'Hara said to wait but I couldn't. I missed you, Daddy! I missed you, Mommy!"

Without waiting for encouragement, she rushed toward them. "I brought you breakfast in bed, just like you always wanted, Daddy. See? I made it myself. I brought you chocolate milk and jelly beans and graham crackers and..."

While she explained the menu, Gable strolled through the doorway, closely followed by platinum Lombard, looking sleek and beautiful. The two cats paused at the foot of the bed as if considering whether or not to make the leap.

Their decision was made for them when Larry bounded into the room, yipping with delight at the sight of the two cats—who landed with a plop in the middle of the velvet coverlet.

Mrs. O'Hara bustled in with Baron trailing along behind. "Good heavens, what's going on here? Shoo, cats! How was the Caribbean, folks? Molly, I told you not to disturb your parents before 1:00 p.m. and it's only twelve. Larry, you miserable cur, get out of here! Shoo, all of you, shoo!"

Garrett sat up, the sheets and coverlet pooling around his waist, revealing his muscular chest. "Hold it! Nobody has to shoo anywhere." He smiled at his bride. "Do they, Mrs. Jackson?"

Brooke rolled over onto her side, propping her head on a hand. "Certainly not, Mr. Jackson. You know, all those times you tried to talk me into breakfast in bed, I might have given in if I'd known you meant it to be a family affair."

Mrs. O'Hara's face turned red. "Well, I never!" She backed toward the door. "You kids have...uh, fun. I've got work to do." She went out, closing the door behind her.

Garrett leaned over to pick Molly up, tray and all, and add her to the tangle of cats and people. "Mrs. O'Hara says to have fun. Think we can do that, pumpkin?"

"Oh, yes, Daddy! Breakfast in bed is lots of fun." And Molly was right; it was.

❖ Harlequin Romance ®

brings you

*Authors you'll treasure,
books you'll want to keep!*

Harlequin Romance just keeps getting better and better...and we're delighted to welcome you to our **Simply the Best** showcase for 1997, highlighting a special author each month!

These are stories we know you'll love reading—again and again! Because they are, quite simply, the best...

Don't miss these unforgettable romances coming to you in May, June and July.

May—GEORGIA AND THE TYCOON (#3455)
by Margaret Way
June—WITH HIS RING (#3459)
by Jessica Steele
July—BREAKFAST IN BED (#3465)
by Ruth Jean Dale

Available wherever Harlequin books are sold.

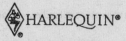

Let's Celebrate!

LOVE & LAUGHTER™

invites you to
the party of the season!

Grab your popcorn and be prepared to laugh
as we celebrate with **LOVE & LAUGHTER**.

Harlequin's newest series is going Hollywood!

Let us make you laugh with three months of terrific
books, authors and romance, plus a chance to win a
FREE 15-copy video collection of the best romantic
comedies ever made.

For more details look in the back pages of any
Love & Laughter title, from July to September,
at your favorite retail outlet.

Don't forget the popcorn!

Available wherever
Harlequin books are sold.

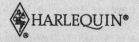

♦ HARLEQUIN®

Harlequin Romance®

is proud to announce the latest arrivals in our bouncing baby series

Each month in 1997 we'll be bringing you your very own bundle of joy—a cute, delightful romance by one of your favorite authors. Our heroes and heroines are about to discover that two's company and three (or four...or five) is a family!

Find out about the true labor of love...

Don't miss these charming stories of parenthood, and how to survive it, coming in May, June and July.

**May—THE SECRET BABY (#3457)
by Day Leclaire
June—FOR BABY'S SAKE (#3461)
by Val Daniels
July—BABY, YOU'RE MINE! (#3463)
by Leigh Michaels**

Available wherever Harlequin books are sold.

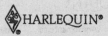

Coming in August 1997!

THE BETTY NEELS
RUBY COLLECTION

August 1997—Stars Through the Mist
September 1997—The Doubtful Marriage
October 1997—The End of the Rainbow
November 1997—Three for a Wedding
December 1997—Roses for Christmas
January 1998—The Hasty Marriage

COLLECTOR'S EDITION

This August start assembling the
Betty Neels Ruby Collection. Six of the
most requested and best-loved titles have
been especially chosen for this collection.
From August 1997 until January 1998,
one title per month will be available to avid
fans. Spot the collection by the lush ruby red
cover with the gold Collector's Edition banner
and your favorite author's name—Betty Neels!

Available in August at your favorite retail outlet.

HARLEQUIN®